Praise for
Doris Lessing's Novella

"Lessing sets the scene instantly, viscerally, and explores the folds and recesses of character with astonishing economy."
—*Boston Globe*

"[Lessing] has a seismographer's feel for the fissures beneath the surface of family and for the tension between personal yearning and society's conventions."
—*Milwaukee Journal Sentinel*

"Intensely readable. . . . [Lessing] offers startling perspectives on domesticity and desire."
—*O, The Oprah Magazine*

"Powerful . . . beautifully realized."   —*Miami Herald*

"A keen sociological eye for class and ideology; an understanding of the contradictory impulses of the human heart; an ability to conjure a place, a mood, and a time through seemingly matter-of-fact descriptions."
—Michiko Kakutani, *New York Times*

"Stunning . . . showing Lessing's trademark incisiveness."
—*Vogue*

ADORE

ADORE

A Novella

DORIS LESSING

HARPER PERENNIAL

NEW YORK • LONDON • TORONTO • SYDNEY • NEW DELHI • AUCKLAND

HARPER PERENNIAL

Cover art used courtesy of Exclusive Media
and © Exclusive Media.

This book is a work of fiction. The characters, incidents, and
dialogue are drawn from the author's imagination and are
not to be construed as real. Any resemblance to actual events
or persons, living or dead, is entirely coincidental.

Originally published as "The Grandmothers" in the collection *The Grandmothers: Four Short Novels* in hardcover in the
United States in 2004 by HarperCollins Publishers.

P.S.™ is a trademark of HarperCollins Publishers.

HarperCollins books may be purchased for educational,
business, or sales promotional use. For information please
e-mail the Special Markets Department at
SPsales@harpercollins.com.

FIRST EDITION

Library of Congress Cataloging-in-Publication Data
has been applied for.

ISBN 978-0-06-231896-1

13 14 15 16 17   OV/RRD   10 9 8 7 6 5 4 3 2 1

ADORE

On either side of a little promontory loaded with cafés and restaurants was a frisky but decorous sea, nothing like the real ocean that roared and rumbled outside the gape of the enclosing bay and barrier rocks known by everyone – and it was even on the charts – as Baxter's Teeth. Who was Baxter? A good question, often asked, and answered by a framed sheet of skilfully antiqued paper on the wall of the restaurant at the end of the promontory, the one in the best, highest and most prestigious position. Baxter's, it was called, claiming that the inner room of thin brick and reed had been Bill Baxter's shack, built by his own hands. He had been a restless voyager, a seaman who had chanced on this paradise of a bay with its little tongue of rocky land. Earlier versions of the tale hinted at pacific and welcoming natives. Where did the Teeth come into it? Baxter remained an inveterate explorer of nearby shores and islands, and then, having entrusted himself to a little leaf of a boat built out of driftwood and expertise, he was wrecked one moony night on those seven black rocks, well within the sight of his little house where a storm lantern, as reliable as a lighthouse, welcomed in ships small enough to get into the bay, having negotiated the reef.

Baxter's was now well planted with big trees that sheltered tables and attendant chairs, and on three sides below was the friendly sea.

A path wandered up through shrubs, coming to a stop in Baxter's Gardens, and one afternoon six people were making the gentle ascent, four adults and two little girls, whose shrieks of pleasure echoed the noises of the gulls.

Two handsome men came first, not young, but only malice could call them middle-aged. One limped. Then two as handsome women of about sixty – but no one would dream of calling them elderly. At a table evidently well-known to them, they deposited bags and wraps and toys, sleek and shining people, as they are who know how to use the sun. They arranged themselves, the women's brown and silky legs ending in negligent sandals, their competent hands temporarily at rest. Women on one side, men on the other, the little girls fidgeting: six fair heads? Surely they were related? Those had to be the mothers of the men; they had to be their sons. The little girls, clamouring for the beach, which was down a rocky path, were told by their grandmothers, and then their fathers, to behave and play nicely. They squatted and made patterns with fingers and little sticks in the dust. Pretty little girls: so they should be with such good-looking progenitors.

From a window of Baxter's a girl called to them, 'The usual? Shall I bring your usual?' One of the women waved to her, meaning yes. Soon appeared a tray where fresh fruit juices and wholemeal sandwiches asserted that these were people careful of their health.

Theresa, who had just taken her school-leaving exams, was on her year away from England, where she would be returning to university. This information had been offered months ago, and in return she was kept up to date with the progress of the little girls at their first school. Now she enquired how school was going along, and first one child and then the other piped up to say their school was cool. The pretty waitress ran back to her station inside Baxter's with a smile at the two men which made the women smile at each other and then at their sons, one of whom, Tom, remarked, 'But she'll never make it back to Britain, all the boys are after her to stay.'

'More fool her if she marries and throws all that away,' said one of the women, Roz – in fact Rozeanne, the mother of Tom. But the other woman, Lil (or Liliane), the mother of Ian, said, 'Oh, I don't know,' and she was smiling at Tom. This concession, or compliment, to their, after all, claim to existence, made the men nod to each other, lips compressed, humorously, as at an often-heard exchange, or one like it.

'Well,' said Roz, 'I don't care, nineteen is too young.'

'But who knows how it might turn out?' enquired Lil, and blushed. Feeling her face hot she made a little grimace, which had the effect of making her seem naughty, or daring, and this was so far from her character that the others exchanged looks not to be explained so easily.

They all sighed, heard each other and now laughed, a full frank laugh that seemed to acknowledge things unsaid. One little girl, Shirley, said, 'What are you laughing at?' and the other, Alice, 'What's so funny? I don't see anything funny,' and copied her grandmother's look of conscious naughtiness, which in fact had not been intended. Lil was uncomfortable and blushed again.

Shirley persisted, wanting attention, 'What's the joke, Daddy?' and at this both daddies began a tussling and buffeting of their daughters, while the girls protested, and ducked, but came back for more, and then fled to their grandmothers' arms and laps for protection. There they stayed, thumbs in their mouths, eyes drooping, yawning. It was a hot afternoon.

A scene of somnolence and satisfaction. At tables all around under the great trees similarly blessed people lazed. The seas all around them, only a few feet below, sighed and hissed and lapped, and the voices were low and lazy.

From the window of Baxter's Theresa stood with a tray of cool drinks momentarily suspended and looked out at the family. Tears slid down her cheeks. She had been in love with Tom and then Ian, and then Tom again, for their looks and their ease, and something, an air of repletion, as if they had been soaking in pleasure all their lives and now gave it out in the form of invisible waves of contentment.

And then the way they handled the little girls, the ease and competence of that. And the way the grandmothers were always available, making the four the six . . . but where were the mothers, children had mothers, and these two little girls had Hannah and Mary, both startlingly unlike the blonde family they had married into, being small and dark, and, while pretty enough, Theresa knew neither of them was good enough for the men. They worked. They owned a business. That is why the grandmothers were so often here. Didn't the grandmothers work, then? Yes, they did but were free to say, 'Let's go to Baxter's' – and up here to Baxter's they came. The mothers too, sometimes, and there were eight.

Theresa was in love with them all. She had at last understood it. The men, yes, her heart ached for them, but not too severely. What made the tears come was seeing them all there, watching them, as she did now. Behind her, at a table near the bar, was Derek, a young farmer who had wished to marry her. She didn't mind him, rather fancied him, but she knew that this, the family, was the real passion.

Over deep layers of tree shadow lanced with sunlight, sun enclosed the tree, the hot blue air, interfused with bliss, happiness, seemed about to exude great drops of something like a golden dew, which only she could see. It was at that moment she decided she would marry her farmer and stay here, on this continent. She could not leave it for the fitful charms of England, of Bradford, though the moors did well enough, when the sun did decide to shine. No, she would stay here, she had to. 'I want it, I want it,' she told herself, allowing the tears at last to run freely. She wanted this physical ease, the calm of it, expressing itself in lazy movements, in long brown legs and arms, and the glint of gold on fair heads where the sun had been.

Just as she claimed her future, she saw one of the mothers coming up the path. Mary – yes, it was. A little dark fidget of a woman, with nothing in her of the poise and style of The Family.

She was coming up slowly. She stopped, stared, went on, stopped, and she was moving with a deliberation that was willed.

'Well, what's got into *her*, I wonder?' mused Theresa, at last leaving her window to take the tray to by now surely impatient customers. Mary Struthers was hardly moving at all. She stood staring at her family, frowning. Roz Struthers saw her and waved, and then again, and while her hand slowly lowered itself, as if caution had made an announcement, her face was already beginning to lose its gloss and glow. She was looking, but as it were indirectly, at her daughter-in-law, and because of what her face was saying, her son Tom turned to look, then wave. Ian, too, waved. Both men's hands fell, as Roz's had done; there was fatality in it.

Mary had stopped. Near her was a table and she collapsed into a chair. Still she stared at Lil, and then at Tom, her husband. From one face to the other those narrowed accusing eyes moved. Eyes that searched for something.

In her hand was a packet. Letters. She sat perhaps ten feet away, staring.

Theresa, having dealt with her other tables, was in her window again, and she was thinking accusing thoughts about Mary, this wife of a son, and she knew it was jealousy. She defended herself thus: But if she was good enough for them, I wouldn't mind her. She's just nothing compared to them.

Only the eye of jealousy could have dismissed Mary, who was a striking, attractive, dark young woman. She wasn't pretty now; her face was small and putty-coloured and her lips were thin. Theresa saw the bundle of letters. She saw the four people at the table. As if they were playing statues, she thought. Light was draining away from them. The splendid afternoon might be brazening it all out but they sat struck, motionless. And still Mary stared, now at Lil, or Liliane, now at Roz or Rozeanne; from them to Tom, and to Ian, and then around again, and again.

From an impulse Theresa did not recognise in herself she poured water from the jug in the fridge into a glass, and ran across with it to Mary. Mary did turn her head slowly to frown into Theresa's face, but did not take the glass. Theresa set it down. Then Mary was attracted by the glitter of the water, reached out her hand for the glass, but withdrew it: her hand was shaking too hard to hold a glass.

Theresa went back to her window. The afternoon had gone dark for her. She was trembling too. What was the matter? What was wrong? Something was horribly, fatally wrong.

At last Mary got up, with difficulty, made the distance to the table where her family sat, and let herself subside into a chair that was away from them: she was not part of them.

Now the four were taking in that bundle of letters in Mary's hand.

They sat quite still, looking at Mary. Waiting.

It was for her to speak. But did she need to? Her lips trembled, she trembled, she appeared to be on the verge of a faint, and those young clear accusing eyes moved still from one face to another. Tom. Lil. Roz. Ian. Her mouth was twisted, as if she had bitten into something sour.

'What's wrong with them, what's wrong?' thought Theresa, staring from her window, and whereas not an hour ago she had decided she could never leave this coast, this scene of pleasantness and plenitude, now she thought, I must get away. I'll tell Derek, no. I want to get out.

Alice, the child on Roz's lap, woke with a cry, saw her mother there, 'Mummy, Mummy,' – and held out her arms. Mary managed to get up, steadied herself around the table on the backs of chairs, and took Alice.

Now it was the other little girl, waking on Lil's lap. 'Where's my mummy?'

Mary held out her hand for Shirley and in a moment both children were on her knees.

The little girls felt Mary's panic, her anger, sensed some

kind of fatality, and now tried to get back to their grandmothers. 'Granny, Granny,' 'I want Granny.'

Mary gripped them both tight.

On Roz's face was a small bitter smile, as if she exchanged confirmation of some bad news with someone
deep inside herself.

'Granny, are you coming to fetch me tomorrow for the
beach?'

And Alice, 'Granny, you promised we would go to the
beach.'

And now Mary spoke at last, her voice shaking. All she
said was, 'No, you will not be going to the beach.' And,
direct to the older women, 'You will not be taking Shirley and Alice to the beach.' That was the judgement and
the sentence.

Lil said tentatively, even humbly, 'I'll see you soon, Alice.'

'No you won't,' said Mary. She stood up, a child on
either hand, the bundle of letters thrust into the pocket of
her slacks. 'No,' she said wildly, the emotion that had been
poisoning her at last pulsing out. 'No. No, you won't. Not
ever. You will not ever see them again.'

She turned to go, pulling the children with her.

Her husband Tom said, 'Wait a minute, Mary.'

'No.' Off she went down the path, as fast as she could,
stumbling and pulling the children along.

And now surely these four remaining, the women and
their sons, should say something, elucidate, make things

clear? Not a word. Pinched, diminished, darkened, they sat on, and then at last one spoke. It was Ian who spoke, direct to Roz, in a passionate intimacy, wild-eyed, his lips stiff and angry.

'It's your fault,' he said. 'Yes, it's your fault. I told you. It's all your fault this has happened.'

Roz met his anger with her own. She laughed. A hard angry bitter laugh, peal after peal. 'My fault,' she said. 'Of course. Who else?' And she laughed. It would have done well on the stage, that laugh, but tears poured down her face.

Out of sight down the path, Mary had reached Hannah, the wife of Ian, who had been unable to face the guilty ones, at least not with Mary, whose rage she could not match. She had let Mary go up by herself and she waited here, full of doubt, misery and reproaches that were beginning to bubble up wanting to overflow. But not in anger, no, she needed explanations. She took Shirley from Mary, and the two young women, their children in their arms, stood together on the path, just outside a plumbago hedge that was the boundary for another café. They did not speak, but looked into each other's faces, Hannah seeking confirmation, which she got. 'It's true, Hannah.'

And now, the laughter. Roz was laughing. The peals of hard laughter, triumphant laughter, was what Mary and Hannah heard, each harsh loud peal lashed them, they shrank away from the cruel sounds. They trembled as the whips of laughter fell.

'Evil,' Mary pronounced at last, through lips that

seemed to have become dough or clay. And as Roz's final yells of laughter reached them, the two young women burst into tears and went running away down the path, away from their husbands, and their husbands' mothers.

Two little girls arrived at the big school on the same day, at the same hour, took each other's measure, and became best friends. Little things, so bravely confronting that great school, as populous and busy as a supermarket, but filled with what they already knew were hierarchies of girls they felt as hostile, but here was an ally, and they stood holding hands, trembling with fear and their efforts to be brave. A great school, standing on its rise, surrounded by parkland in the English manner, but arched over by a most un-English sky, about to absorb these little things, babies really, their four parents thought – enough to bring tears to their eyes! – and they did.

They were doughty, quick with repartee, and soon lived down the bullying that greeted new girls; they stood up for each other, fought their own and each other's battles. 'Like sisters,' people said, and even, 'Like twins.' Fair, they were, with their neat gleaming ponytails, both of them, and blue-eyed, and as quick as fishes, but really, if you looked, not so alike. Liliane – or Lil – was thin, with a hard little body, her features delicate, and Rozeanne – Roz – was sturdier, and where Lil regarded the world with a pure severe gaze, Roz found jokes in everything. But it is nice to think, and say, 'like sisters', 'they might be twins'; it is agreeable to find resemblances where perhaps none are, and so it went on, through the school terms and the years, two girls, inseparable, which was nice for their families, living in the same street, with parents who had become friends because of them, as so often happens, knowing they were lucky in their girls choosing each other and making lives easy for everyone.

But these lives were easy. Not many people in the world have lives so pleasant, unproblematical, unreflecting: no one on these blessed coasts lay awake and wept for their sins, or for money, let alone for food. What a good-looking lot, smooth and shiny with sun, with sport, with good food. Few people anywhere know of coasts like these, except perhaps for brief holidays, or in travellers' tales like dreams. Sun and sea, sea and sun, and always the sound of waves on beaches.

It was a blue world the little girls grew up in. At the end of every street was the sea, as blue as their eyes – as they were told often enough. Over their heads the blue sky was so seldom louring or grey that such days were enjoyable for their rarity. A rare harsh wind brought the pleasant sting of salt and the air was always salty. The little girls would lick the salt from their own hands and arms and from each other's too, in a game they called, 'Playing puppies'. Bedtime baths were always salty so that they had to shower off the bath water with water coming from deep in the earth and tasting of minerals, not salt. When Roz stayed over at Lil's house, or Lil at Roz's, the parents would stand smiling down at the two pretty imps cuddled together like kittens or puppies, smelling now they were asleep not of salt but of soap. And always, throughout their childhoods, day and night, the sound of the sea, the gentle tamed waves of Baxter's sea, a hushing and a lulling, like breathing.

Sisters, or, for that matter, twins, even best friends, suffer passionate rivalries, often concealed, even from each other. But Roz knew how Lil grieved when her breasts – Roz's – popped forth a good year before Lil's, not to mention other evidences of growing up, and she was generous in assurances and comfort, knowing that her own deep envy of her friend was not going to be cured by time. She wished that her own body could be as hard and thin as Lil's, who wore her clothes with such style and ease, whereas she was already being called – by the unkind – plump. She had to be careful what she ate, whereas Lil could eat what she liked.

So there they were, quite soon, teenagers, Lil the athlete, excelling in every sport, and Roz in the school plays, with big parts, making people laugh, extrovert, large, vital, loud: they complemented each other as once they had been as like as two peas: 'You can hardly tell them apart.'

They both went to university, Lil because of the sport, Roz because of the theatre group, and they remained best friends, sharing news about their conquests, and making light of their rivalries, but their closeness was such that although they starred in such different arenas, their names were always coupled. Neither went in for the great excluding passions, broken hearts, jealousies.

And now that was it, university done with, here was the grown-up world, and this was a culture where girls married young. 'Twenty and still not married!'

Roz began dating Harold Struthers, an academic, and a bit of a poet, too; and Lil met Theo Western, who owned a sports equipment and clothes shop. Rather, shops. He was well off. The men got on – the women were careful that they did, and there was a double wedding.

So far so good.

Those shrimps, the silverfish, the minnows, were now wonderful young women, one in a wedding dress like an arum lily (Liliane) and Roz's like a silver rose. So judged the main fashion page of the big paper.

They lived in two houses in a street running down to the sea, not far from the outspit of land that held Baxter's, unfashionable but artistic, and, by that law that says if you want to know if an area is going up, then look to see if those early swallows, the artists, are moving in, it would not be unfashionable for long. They were on opposite sides of the street.

Lil was a swimming champion known over the whole continent and abroad too, and Roz not only acted and sang, but was putting on plays and began devising shows and spectacles. Both were very busy. Despite all this Liliane and Theo Western announced the birth of Ian, and Rozeanne and Harold Struthers followed within a week with Thomas.

Two little boys, fair-haired and delightful, and people said they could be brothers. In fact Tom was a solid little boy easily embarrassed by the exuberances of his mother, and Ian was fine drawn and nervy and 'difficult' in ways Tom never was. He did not sleep well, and sometimes had nightmares.

The two families spent weekends and holidays together, one big happy family, as Roz sang, defining the situation, and the two men might go off on trips into the mountains or to fish, or backpacking. Boys will be boys, as Roz said.

All this went on, and anything that was not what it should be was kept well out of sight. 'If it ain't broke, don't fix it,' Roz might say. She was concerned for Lil, for reasons that will emerge, but not for herself. Lil might have her problems, but not she, not she and Harold and Tom. Everything was going along fine.

And then this happened.

The scene: the connubial bedroom, when the boys were about ten. Roz lay sprawling on the bed, Harold sat on the arm of a chair, looking at his wife, smiling, but determined. He had just said he had been offered a professorship, in a university in another state.

Roz said, 'Well, I suppose you can come down for weekends or we can come up.'

This was so like her, the dismissal of a threat – surely? – to their marriage, that he gave a short, not unaffectionate laugh, and after a pause said, 'I want you and Tom to come too.'

'Move from *here*?' And Roz sat up shaking her fair and now curly head so that she could see him clearly. '*Move*?'

'Why don't you just say it? Move from Lil, that's the point, isn't it?'

Roz clasped her hands together on her upper chest, all theatrical consternation. But she was genuinely astounded, indignant.

'What are you suggesting?'

'I'm not suggesting. I'm saying. Strange as it may seem . . .' – This phrase usually signals strife – 'I'd like a wife. A real one.'

'You're mad.'

'No. I want you to watch something.' He produced a canister of film. 'Please, Roz. I mean it. I want you to come next door and watch this.'

Up got Roz, off the bed, all humorous protest.

She was all but nude. With a deep sigh, aimed at the gods, or some impartial viewer, she put on a pink feathered negligee, salvaged from a play's wardrobe: she had felt it was so *her*.

She sat in the next room, opposite a bit of white wall kept clear of clutter. 'And now what are you up to, I wonder?' she said, amiably. 'You big booby, Harold. *Really*, I mean, I ask you!'

Harold began running the film – home movies. It was of the four of them, two husbands, the two women. They had been on the beach, and wore wraps over bikinis. The men were still in their swimming trunks. Roz and Lil sat on the sofa, this sofa, where Roz now was, and the men were in hard upright chairs, sitting forward to watch. The women were talking. What about? Did it matter? They were watching each other's faces, coming in quickly to make a point. The men kept trying to intervene, join in, the women literally did not hear them. Harold, then Theo, was annoyed, and they raised their voices, but the women still did not hear, and when at last the men shouted, insisting, Roz put out a hand to stop them.

Roz remembered the discussion, just. It was not important. The boys were to go to a friend's for a weekend camp. The parents were discussing it, that was all. In fact the mothers were discussing it, the fathers might just as well not have been there.

The men had been silenced, sat watching and even exchanged looks. Harold was annoyed, but Theo's demeanour said only, *'Women, what do you expect?'*

And then, that subject disposed of – the boys – Roz said, 'I simply must tell you . . .' and leaned forward to tell Lil, dropping her voice, not knowing she did this, telling her something, nothing important.

The husbands sat and watched, Harold all alert irony, Theo bored.

It went on. The tape ran out.

'Do you mean to say you actually filmed that – to trap me? You set it up, to get at me!'

'No, don't you remember? I had made a film of the boys on the beach. Then you took the camera and filmed me and Theo. And then Theo said, "How about the girls?"'

'Oh,' said Roz.

17

'Yes. It was only when I played it back later – yesterday, in fact, that I saw . . . Not that I was surprised. That's how it always is. It's you and Lil. Always.'

'What are you suggesting? Are you saying we're lezzies?'

'No. I'm not. And what difference would it make if you were?'

'I simply don't get it.'

'Obviously sex doesn't matter that much. We have, I think, more than adequate sex, but it's not me you have the relationship with.'

Roz sat, all twisted with emotion, wringing her hands, the tears ready to start.

'And so I want you to come with me up north.'

'You must be mad.'

'Oh, I know you won't, but you could at least pretend to think about it.'

'Are you suggesting we divorce?'

'I wasn't, actually. If I found a woman who put me first then . . .'

'You'd let me know!' she said, all tears at last.

'Oh, Roz,' said her husband. 'Don't think I'm not sorry. I'm fond of you, you know that. I'll miss you like crazy. You're my pal. And you're the best lay I'm ever likely to have and I know that too. But I feel like a sort of shadow here. I don't matter. That's all.'

And now it was his turn to blink away tears and then put his hands up to his eyes. He went back to the bedroom, lay down on the bed, and she joined him. They comforted each other. 'You're mad, Harold, do you know that? I love you.' 'And I love you too Roz, don't think that I don't.'

Then Roz asked Lil to come over, and the two women watched the film, without speaking, to its end.

'And that's why Harold is leaving me,' said Roz, who had told Lil the outlines of the situation.

'I don't see it,' said Lil at last, frowning with the effort of trying. She was deadly serious, and Roz serious but smiling and angry.

'Harold says my real relationship is with you, not with him.'

'What does he want, then?' asked Lil.

'He says you and I made him feel excluded.'

'*He* feel excluded! I've always felt – left out. All these years I've been watching you and Harold and I've wished . . .' Loyalty had locked her tongue until this moment, but now she came out with it at last: 'I have a lousy marriage. I have a bad time with Theo. I've never . . . but you knew. And you and Harold, always so happy . . . I don't know how often I've left you two here and gone home with Theo and wished . . .'

'I didn't know . . . I mean, I did know, of course, Theo isn't the ideal husband.'

'You can say that again.'

'It seems to me it's you who should be getting a divorce.'

'Oh, no, no,' said Lil, warding off the idea with an agitated hand. 'No; I once said in joke to Ian – testing him out, what he'd think if I got a divorce and he nearly went berserk. He was silent for such a long time – you know how he goes silent, and then he shouted and began crying. "You can't," he said. "You can't. I won't let you."'

'So poor Tom is going to be without a father,' said Roz.

'And Ian doesn't have much of one,' said Lil. And then, when it could seem the conversation was at an end, she enquired, 'Roz, did Harold say that we are lezzies?'

'All but – well no, not exactly.'

'Is that what he meant?'

'I don't know. I don't think so.' Roz was suffering now with the effort of this unusual and unwonted introspection. 'I don't understand, I told him. I don't understand what you're on about.'

'Well, we aren't, are we?' enquired Lil, apparently needing to be told.

'Well, I don't think we are,' said Roz.

'We've always been friends, though.'

'Yes.'

'When did it start? I remember the first day at school.'

'Yes.'

'But before that? How did it happen?'

'I can't remember. Perhaps it was just – luck.'

'You can say that again. The luckiest thing in my life – you.'

'Yes,' said Roz. 'But that doesn't make us . . . Bloody men,' she said, suddenly energetic and brisk with anger.

'Bloody men,' said Lil, with feeling, because of her husband.

This note, obligatory for that time, having been struck, the conversation was over.

Off went Harold to his university which was surrounded, not by ocean and sea winds and the songs and tales of the sea, but by sand, scrub and thorns. Roz visited him, and then returned there to put on *Oklahoma!* – a great success – and they enjoyed their more than adequate sex. She said, 'I don't see what you're complaining about,' and he said, 'Well, no, you wouldn't, would you?' When he came down to visit her and the boys – who being always together were always referred to in the plural – nothing seemed to have changed. As a family they went about, the amiable Harold and the exuberant Roz, a popular young couple – perhaps not so young now – as described often in the gossip columns. For a marriage that had been given its notice to quit the two seemed no less of a couple. As they jested – jokes had never been in short supply – they were like those trees whose centre has rotted away, or the bushes spreading from the centre, which disappear as its suburbs spring up. It was so hard for this couple to fray apart. Everywhere they went, his old pupils greeted him and people who had been involved in one of her productions greeted her. They were Harold and Roz to hundreds of people. 'Do you remember me – Roz, Harold?' She always did and Harold knew his old pupils. Like Royalty who expect of themselves that they remember faces and names. 'The Struthers are separating? Oh, come on! I don't believe it.'

And now the other couple, no less in the limelight,

Lil always judging swimming or running or other sports events, bestowing prizes, making speeches. And there too was the handsome husband, Theo, known for the chain of sports equipment and clothes shops. The two lean, good-looking people, on view, like their friends, the other couple, but so different in style. Nothing excessive or exuberant about them, they were affable, smiling, available, the very essence of good citizenship.

The break-up of Roz and Harold did not disrupt Theo and Lil. The marriage had been a façade for years. Theo had a succession of girls, but, as he complained, he couldn't get into his bed anywhere without finding a girl in it: he travelled a lot, for the firm.

Then Theo was killed in a car crash, and Lil was a well-off widow, with her boy Ian, the moody one, so unlike Tom, and in that seaside town, where the climate and the style of living put people so much on view, there were two women, without men, and their two little boys.

The young couple with their children: interesting that, the turning point, the moment of change. For a time, seen, commented on, a focus, the young parents, by definition sexual beings, and tagging along or running around them the pretty children. 'Oh, what a lovely little boy, what a pretty little girl, What's your name? – what a nice name!' – and then all at once, or so it seems, the parents, no longer quite so young, seem to lose height a little, even to shrink, they certainly lose colour and lustre. 'How old did you say he is, she is . . .' The young ones are shooting up and glamour has shifted its quarters. Eyes are following them, rather than the parents. 'They do grow up so fast these days, don't they?'

The two good-looking women, together again as if men had not entered their equation at all, went about with the two beautiful boys, one rather delicate and poetic with sun-burnished locks falling over his forehead, and the other strong and athletic, friends, as their mothers had been at that age. There was a father in the picture, Harold, up north, but he'd shacked up with a young woman who presumably did not suffer from Roz's deficiencies. He came to visit, and stayed in Roz's house, but not in the bedroom (which had to strike both partners as absurd), and Tom visited him in his university. But the reality was, two women in their mid-thirties, and two lads who were not far off being young men. The houses, so close, opposite each other, seemed to belong to both families. 'We are an extended family,' cried Roz, not one to let a situation remain undefined.

The beauty of young boys — now, that isn't an easy thing. Girls, yes, full of their enticing eggs, the mothers of us all, that makes sense, they should be beautiful and usually are, even if only for a year or a day. But boys — why? What for? There is a time, a short time, at about sixteen, seventeen, when they have a poetic aura. They are like young gods. Their families and their friends may be awed by these beings who seem visitors from a finer air. They are often unaware of it, seeming to themselves more like awkwardly packed parcels they are trying to hold together.

Roz and Lil lolled on the little verandah overlooking the sea, and saw the two boys come walking up the path, frowning a little, dangling swimming things they would put to dry on the verandah wall, and they were so beautiful the two women sat up to look at each other, sharing incredulity. 'Good God!' said Roz. 'Yes,' said Lil. '*We* made that, *we* made them,' said Roz. 'If we didn't, who did?' said Lil. And the boys, having disposed of their towels and trunks, went past with smiles that indicated they were busy on their own affairs: they did not want to be summoned for food or to tidy their beds, or something equally unimportant.

'My God!' said Roz again. 'Wait, Lil . . .' She got up and went inside, and Lil waited, smiling a little to herself, as she often did, at her friend's dramatic ways. Out came Roz with a book in her hand, a photograph album. She pushed her chair against Lil's, and together they turned the pages past babies on rugs, babies in baths – themselves, then 'her first step' and 'the first tooth' – and they were at the page they knew they both sought. Two girls, at about sixteen.

'My God!' said Roz.

'We didn't do too badly, then,' said Lil.

Pretty girls, yes, very, all sugar and spice, but if photographs were taken now of Ian and Tom, would they show the glamour that stopped the breath when one saw them walk across a room or saunter up out of the waves?

They lingered over the pages of themselves, in this album, Roz's; Lil's would have to be the same. Photographs of Roz, with Lil. Two pretty girls.

24

What they were looking for they did not find. Nowhere could they find the shine of unearthliness that illuminated their two sons, at this time.

And there they were sitting, the album spread out across both their stretched-out brown legs – they were in bikinis – when the boys came out, glasses of fruit juice in their hands.

They sat on the wall of the verandah's edge and contemplated their mothers, Roz and Lil.

'What are they doing?' Ian seriously asked Tom.

'What are they doing?' echoed Tom, owlishly, joking as always. He jumped up, peered down at the open page, half on Roz's, half on Lil's knees, and returned to his place. 'They are admiring their beauty when they were nymphets,' he reported to Ian. 'Aren't you, Ma?' he said to Roz.

'That's right,' said Roz. 'Tempus fugit. It fugits like anything. You have no idea – yet. We wanted to find out what we were like all those years ago.'

'Not so many years,' said Lil.

'Don't bother to count,' said Roz. 'Enough years.'

Now Ian captured the album off the women's thighs, and he and Tom sat staring at the girls, their mothers.

'They weren't bad,' said Tom to Ian.

'Not bad at all,' said Ian to Tom.

The women smiled at each other: more of a grimace.

'But you are better now,' said Ian, and went red.

'Oh, you are charming,' said Roz, accepting the compliment for herself.

'I don't know,' said the clown, Tom, pretending to compare the old photographs with the two women sitting there, in their bikinis. 'I don't know. Now? –' and he screwed up his eyes for the examination. 'And then.' He bent to goggle at the photographs.

'Now has it,' he pronounced. 'Yes, better now.' And at this the two boys fell to foot-and-shoulder wrestling, or jostling, as they often still did, like boys, though what people saw were young gods who couldn't take a step or make a gesture that was not from some archaic vase, or antique dance.

'Our mothers,' said Tom, toasting them in orange juice.

'Our mothers,' said Ian, smiling directly at Roz in a way that made her shift about in her chair and move her legs.

Roz had said to Lil that Ian had a crush on her, Roz, and Lil had said, 'Well, never mind, he'll get over it.'

What Ian was not getting over, had not begun to get over, was his father's death, already a couple of years behind, in time. From the moment he had ceased to have a father he had pined, becoming thinner, almost transparent, so that his mother complained, 'Do eat, Ian, eat something – you must.'

'Oh, leave me alone.'

It was all right for Tom, whose father turned up sometimes, and whom he visited up there in his landlocked university. But Ian had nothing, not even warming memories. Where his father should have been, unsatisfactory as he had been with his affairs and his frequent absences, was nothing, a blank, and Ian tried to put a brave face on it, had bad dreams, and both women's hearts ached for him.

A big boy, his eyes heavy with crying, he would go to his mother, where she sat on a sofa, and collapse beside her, and she would put her arms around him. Or go to Roz, and she embraced him, 'Poor Ian.'

And Tom watched this, seriously, coming to terms with this grief, not his own, but its presence so close in his friend, his almost brother, Ian. 'They are like brothers,' people said. 'Those two, they might as well be brothers.' But in one a calamity was eating away, like a cancer, and not in the other, who tried to imagine the pain of grief and failed.

One night, Roz got up out of her bed to fetch herself a drink from the fridge. Ian was in the house, staying the night with Tom, as so often happened. He would use the second bed in Tom's room, or Harold's room, where he was now. Roz heard him crying and without hesitation went in to put her arms around him, cuddled him like a small boy, as after all she had been doing all his life. He went to sleep in her arms and in the morning his looks at her were demanding, hungry, painful. Roz was silent, contemplating the events of the night. She did not tell Lil what had happened. But what had happened? Nothing that had not a hundred times before. But it was odd. 'She didn't want to worry her!' Really? When had she ever been inhibited from telling Lil everything?

It happened that Tom was over at Lil's house, across the street, with Ian, for a couple of nights. Roz alone, telephoned Harold, and they had an almost connubial chat.

'How's Tom?'

'Oh, he's fine. Tom's always fine. But Ian's not too good. He really is taking Theo's death hard.'

'Poor kid, he'll get over it.'

'He's taking his time, then. Listen, Harold, next time you come perhaps you could take out Ian by himself?'

'What about Tom?'

'Tom'd understand. He's worried about Ian, I know.'

'Right. I'll do that. Count on me.'

And Harold did come, and did take Ian off for a long walk along the sea's edge, and Ian talked to Harold, whom he had known all his life, more like a second father.

'He's very unhappy,' Harold reported to Roz and to Lil.

'I know he is,' said Lil.

'He thinks he's no good. He thinks he's a failure.'

The adults stared at this fact, as if it were something they could actually see.

'But how can you be a failure at seventeen?' said Lil.

'Did we feel like that?' asked Roz.

'I know I did,' said Harold. 'Don't worry.' And back he went to his desert university. He was thinking of getting married again.

'Okay,' said Roz. 'If you want a divorce.'

'Well, I suppose she'll want kids,' said Harold.

'Don't you know?'

'She's twenty-five,' said Harold. 'Do I have to ask?'

'Ah,' said Roz, seeing it all. 'You don't want to put the idea into her head?' She laughed at him.

'I suppose so,' said Harold.

Then Ian was again spending the night with Tom. Rather, he was there at bedtime. He went off to Harold's room, and there was a quick glance at Roz, which she hoped Tom had not seen.

When she woke in the night, ready to go off to the fridge for a drink, or just to wander about the house in the dark, as she often did, she did not go, afraid of hearing Ian crying, afraid she would not be able to stop herself going in to him. But then she found he had blundered through the dark into her room and was beside her, clutching at her like a lifebelt in a storm. And she actually found her-self picturing those seven black rocks like rotten teeth in the black night out there, the waves pouring and dashing around them in white cascades of foam.

Next morning Roz was sitting at the table in the room that was open to the verandah, and the sea air, and the wash and hush and lull of the sea. Tom stumbled in fresh from his bed, the smell on him of youthful sleep. 'Where's Ian?' he asked. Normally he would not have asked: both boys could sleep until midday.

Roz stirred her coffee, around and around, and said, without looking at him, 'He's in my bed.'

This normally would not have merited much notice, since this extended family's casual ways could accommodate mothers and boys, or the women, or either boy with either woman, lying down for a rest or a chat, or the two boys, and, when he was around, Harold with any of them.

Tom stared at her over his still-empty plate.

Roz accepted that look, and her look back might as well have been a nod.

'Jesus!' said Tom.

'Exactly,' said Roz.

And then Tom ignored his plate and possible orange juice, leaped up, grabbed his swimming-trunks from the verandah wall, and he sprinted off down to the sea. Usually he would have yelled at Ian to go too.

Tom was not around that day. It was school holidays, but apparently he was off on some school holiday activity, generally scorned by him.

Lil was away, judging some sports competition, and was not back until evening. She came into Roz's house and said, 'Roz, I'm whacked. Is there anything to eat?'

Ian was at the table, sitting across from Roz but not looking at her. Tom had a plate of food in front of him. And now Tom began talking to Lil as if no one else was there. Lil scarcely noticed this, she was so tired, but the other two did. And he kept it up until the meal was over and Lil said she must go to bed, she was exhausted, and Tom simply got up and went with her into the dark.

Next morning, lateish for them all, Tom walked back across the street and found Roz at the table, in her usual careless, comfortable pose, her wrap loose about her. He did not look at her but all around her, at the room, the ceiling, through a delirium of happy accomplishment.

Roz did not have to guess at his condition; she knew it, because Ian's similar state had been enveloping her all night.

Now Tom was prowling around the room, taking swipes as he passed at a chair arm, the table, a wall, returning to aim a punch at the chair next to hers, like a schoolboy unable to contain exuberance, but then standing to stare in front of him, frowning, thinking – like an adult. Then he whirled about and was close to his mother, all schoolboy, an embodied snigger, a leer. And then trepidation – he was not sure of himself, nor of his mother, who blushed scarlet, went white, and then got up and deliberately slapped him hard, this way, that way, across the face.

'Don't you dare,' she whispered, trembling with rage. 'How dare you . . .'

Half crouching, hands to his head, protecting it, he peered up at her, face distorted in what could have been a schoolboy's blubbering, but then he took command of himself, stood and said directly to her, 'I'm sorry,' though neither he nor she could have said exactly what it was he was sorry for, nor what he was not to dare. Not to let words, or his face, say what he had learned of women in the night just passed, with Lil?

He sat down, put his face in his hands, then leaped up, grabbed his swimming things and was off running into the sea, which this morning was a flat blue plate rimmed by the colourful houses of the enclosing arm of the bay opposite.

Tom did not come into his mother's house that day but made a detour back to Lil's. Ian slept late – nothing new in that. He, too, found it hard to look at her, but she knew it was the sight of her, so terribly familiar, so terribly and newly revelatory, it was too much, and so he snatched up his bundle of swimming things and was off. He did not come back until dark. She had done small tasks, made routine telephone calls, cooked, stood soberly scanning the house opposite, which showed no signs of life, and then, when Ian returned, made them both supper and they went back to bed, locking the house front and back – which was something not always remembered.

A week passed. Roz was sitting alone at the table with a cup of tea when there was a knock. She could not ignore it, she knew that, though she would have liked to stay inside this dream or enchantment that had so unexpectedly consumed her. She had dragged on jeans and a shirt, so she was respectable to look at, at least. She opened the door on the friendly, enquiring face of Saul Butler, who lived some doors along from Lil, and was their good neighbour. He was here because he fancied Lil and wanted her to marry him.

When he sat down and accepted tea, she waited.

'Haven't seen much of you lot recently, and I can't get any reply at Lil's.'

'Well, it's the school holidays.'

But usually she and the boys, Lil and the boys, would have been in and out, and often people waved at them from the street, where they all sat around the table.

'That boy, Ian, he needs a father,' he challenged her.

'Yes, he does,' she agreed at once: she had learned in the past week just how much the boy needed a father.

'I'm pretty sure I'd be a father to Ian – as much as he'd let me.'

Saul Butler was a well-set-up man of about fifty, not looking his age. He ran a chain of artists' equipment shops, paints, canvases, frames, all that kind of thing, and he knew Lil from working with her on the town's trade associations. Roz and Lil had agreed he would make a fine husband, if either of them had been looking for one.

She said, as she had before, 'Shouldn't you be saying this to Lil?'

'But I do. She must be sick of me – staking my claim.'

'And you want me to support – your claim?'

'That's about it. I think I'm a pretty good proposition,' he said, smiling, mocking his own boasting.

'I think you'd be a good proposition too,' said Roz, laughing, enjoying the flirtation, if that was what it was. A week of love-making, and she was falling into the flirtatious mode as if into a bed. 'But that's no use is it, it's Lil you want.'

'Yes. I've had my eye on Lil for – a long time.' This meant, before his wife left him for another man. 'Yes. But she only laughs at me. Now, why is that, I wonder? I'm a very serious sort of chap. And where are the lads this morning?'

'Swimming, I suppose.'

33

'I only dropped in to make sure you are all getting along all right.' He got up, finished his tea standing, and said, 'See you on the beach.'

Off he went and Roz rang Lil, and said, 'We've got to be seen about a bit more. Saul dropped in.'

'I suppose so,' said Lil, her voice heavy, and low.

'We should be seen on the beach, all four of us.'

A hot morning. The sea shimmered off light. The sky was full of a light that could punish the eyes, without dark defending glasses. Lil and Roz, in loose wraps over their bikinis, slathered with suncream, made their way behind the boys to the beach. It was a well-used beach, but at this hour, on a weekday, there were few people. Two chairs, set close against Roz's fence, were faded and battered by storm and sun, but serviceable, and there the women sat themselves. The boys had gone running into the sea. Tom had scarcely greeted his mother; Ian's look at Lil slid off her and away.

The waves were brisk enough for pleasure, but in here, in the bay, were never big enough for surfing, which went on outside, past the Teeth. For all the years of the boys' childhood they played safe, on this beach, but now they saw it as good enough for a swim, and for the serious dangerous stuff they went out onto the surfers' beaches. The two were swimming well apart, ignoring each other, and the women's eyes were behind the secretive dark glasses, and neither wanted to talk – could not.

They saw a head like a seal's quite far out grow larger,

and then it was Saul, and he came out of the sea, waving at them, but went up through the salty sea bushes and past the houses up to the street.

The boys were swimming in. When they reached the shallows they stood up and faced each other. They began to tussle. Thus had they fought all through their growing-up, boy fashion, but soon it was evident that there was nothing childlike about this fight. They were standing waist deep, waves came rushing in, battering them with foam, and streamed away, and then Ian had disappeared and Tom was holding him down. A wave came in, another, and Lil started up in anguish and said, 'Oh, my God, he's going to kill Ian. Tom's going to kill . . .'

Ian reappeared, gasping, clutching Tom's shoulders. Down he went again.

'Be quiet, Lil,' said Roz. 'We mustn't interfere.'

'He's going to kill . . . Tom wants to kill . . .'

Then Ian had been down a long time, surely a minute, more . . .

Tom let out a great yell and let go of Ian, who bobbed up. He was hardly able to stand, fell, stood up again, and watched Tom striding through the waves to the beach. As Tom stepped up onto the sand, blood flowed from his calf. Ian had bitten him, deep under the waves, and it was a bad bite. Ian was standing swaying in the water, choking, gasping.

Roz fought with herself, then ran out into the waves and supported Ian in. The boy was pale, vomiting sea water, but he shook off Roz and went to sit by himself on the sand, his head on his knees. Roz returned to her place. 'Our fault,' whispered Lil.

'Stop it, Lil. That's not going to help.'

Tom was standing on one leg, to examine his calf, which was pouring copious blood. He went back into the sea and stood sloshing the sea water on to the bite. He came out again, found his swimming towel, tore it in half, and tied one half tight around his leg. Then he stood, hesitating. He might have gone back into his house and through it to Lil's. He might have stayed in his own house, claiming it from Ian? He could have flopped down where he stood near the fence, not far from the women. Instead he turned and stared hard, it seemed with curiosity, at Ian. Then he limped to where Ian sat, and sat down by him. No one spoke.

The women stared at these two young heroes, their sons, their lovers, these beautiful young men, their bodies glistening with sea water and sun oil, like wrestlers from an older time.

'What are we going to do, Roz?' whispered Lil.

'I know what I am going to do,' said Roz, and stood up. 'Lunch,' she called, exactly as she had been doing for years, and the boys obediently got up and followed the women into Roz's house.

'You'd better get that dressed,' said Roz to her son. It was Ian who fetched the box of bandages and Elastoplast and put disinfectant on the bite, and then tied up the wound.

On the table was the usual spread of sausages and cheese and ham and bread, a big dish of fruit, and the four sat around the table and ate. Not a word. And then Roz spoke calmly, deliberately. 'We all have to behave normally. Remember – everything must be as usual, as it always is.'

The boys looked at each other, for information, it seemed. They looked at Lil. They looked at Roz. They frowned. Lil was smiling, but only just. Roz cut an apple into four, pushed a quarter each at the others, and bit juicily into her segment.

'*Very* funny,' said Ian.

'I think so,' said Roz.

Ian got up, clutching a big sandwich stuffed with salad, the apple quarter in his other hand, and went into Roz's room.

'*Well*,' said Lil, laughing with something like bitterness.

'Exactly,' said Roz.

Tom got up, and went out and across the street to Lil's house.

'What are we going to do?' Lil asked her friend, as if she expected an answer, there and then.

'It seems to me we are doing it,' said Roz. She followed Ian into her bedroom.

Lil collected up the box with the medicaments and bandages, and walked across to her house. On the way she waved to Saul Butler, who was on his verandah.

School began: it was the boys' last year. Both were prefects, and admired. Lil was often in other towns and places, judging, giving prizes, making speeches, a well-known figure, this slim, tall, shy woman, in her pale perfect linens, her fair hair smooth and neat. She was known for her kind smile, her sympathy, her warmth. Girls and boys had crushes on her and wrote letters that often included, 'I know that you would understand me.' Roz was supervising productions of musicals at a couple of schools, and working on a play, a farce, about sex, a magnetic noisy woman who insisted that her bite was much worse than her bark: 'So watch out; don't make me angry!' The four were in and out, together or separately, nothing seemed to have changed, they ate their meals with windows open on the street, they swam, but sometimes were by themselves on the beach because the boys were out surfing, leaving them behind.

Both had changed, Ian more than Tom. Diffident, shy and awkward he had been, but now he was confident, adult. Roz, who remembered the anguished boy when he had first come to her bed, was quietly proud, but she could never of course say a word to anyone, not even Lil. She had made a man of him, all right. Look at him . . . never these days did he clutch and cling and weep, because of his loneliness and his vanished father. He was quietly proprietorial with her, which amused her – and she adored it. Tom, who had never suffered from shyness or self-doubt, had become a strong, thoughtful youth, who was protective of Lil in a way that Roz had not seen. These were no longer boys, but young men, and good-looking, and so the girls were after them, and both Lil's house and Roz's

38

were, they joked – like fortresses against delirious and desirous young women. But inside these houses, open to sun, sea breezes, the sounds of the sea, were rooms where no one went but Ian and Roz, Tom and Lil.

Lil said to Roz she was so happy it made her afraid. 'How could anything possibly be as wonderful?' she whispered, afraid to be overheard – by whom? No one was anywhere near. What she meant was, and Roz knew she did, that such an intense happiness must have its punishment. Roz grew loud and jokey and said that this was a love that dare not speak its name, and sang, 'I love you, yes I do, I love you, it's a sin to tell a lie . . .'

'Oh, Roz,' said Lil, 'sometimes I get so afraid.'

'Nonsense,' said Roz. 'Don't worry. They'll soon get bored with the old women and go after girls their own age.'

Time passed.

Ian went to college and learned business and money and computers, and worked in the sports firms, helping Lil: soon he would take his father's place. Tom decided to go into theatre management. The best course in the whole country was in his father's university, and it seemed obvious that there was where he should go. Harold wrote and rang to say that there was plenty of room in the house he now shared with his new wife, his new daughter. Harold and Roz had divorced, without acrimony. But Tom said he would stay here, this town was his home, he didn't want to go north. There was a good enough course right here, and besides, his mother was an education in herself. Harold actually made the trip to argue with his son, planning to say that Tom's not wanting to leave home was a sign of his becoming a real mummy's boy, but when he actually confronted Tom, this self-possessed and decided young man, much older than his real age, he could not bring out the evidently unjust accusation. While Harold was staying, several days, Ian had to stay home, and Tom too, in his own house, and none of the four liked this. Harold was conscious they wanted him to leave; he was not wanted. He was uneasy, he was uncomfortable, and said to Roz that surely the two boys were too old to be so often with the older women. 'Well, we haven't got them on leashes,' said Roz. 'They're free to come and go.'

'Well, I don't know,' said Harold, in the end, defeated. And he went back to his new family.

Tom enrolled for theatre management, stage management, stage lighting, costume design, the history of the theatre. The course would take three years.

'We're all working like dogs,' said Roz, loudly to Harold on the telephone. 'I don't know what you're complaining about.'

'You should get married again,' said Roz's ex-husband.

'Well, if you couldn't stand me, then who could?' demanded Roz.

'Oh, Roz, it's just that I am an old-fashioned family man. And you must admit you don't exactly fit that bill.'

'Look. You ditched me. You've got yourself your ideal wife. Now, leave me alone. Get out of my life, Harold.'

'I hope you don't really mean that.'

Meanwhile, Saul Butler courted Lil.

It became a bit of a joke for all of them, Saul too. He would arrive with flowers and sweets, magazines, a poster, when he had seen Lil go into Roz's, and call out, 'Here comes old faithful.' The women made a play of it all, Roz sometimes pretending the flowers were for her. He also visited Lil in her house, leaving at once if Tom were there, or Ian.

'No,' said Lil, 'I'm sorry, Saul. I just don't see myself married again.'

'But you're getting older, Lil. You're getting on. And here is old faithful. You'll be glad of him one day.' Or he said to Roz, 'Lil'll be glad of a man about the place, one of these days.'

One day the boys, or young men, were readying themselves to go out to the big ocean for surfing, when Saul arrived, with flowers for both women. 'Now, you two, sit down,' he said. And the women, smiling, sat and waited.

The boys on the verandah over the sea were collecting surfboards, towels, goggles. 'Hi, Saul,' said Tom. A long pause before Ian's, 'Hello, Saul.' That meant that Tom had nudged Ian into the greeting.

Ian resented and feared Saul. He had said to Roz, 'He wants to take Lil away from us.' 'You mean, from you.' 'Yes. And he wants to get me too. A ready-made son. Why doesn't he make his own kids?'

'I thought I had got you,' said Roz.

At which Ian leaped at her, or on her, demonstrating who had got whom.

'Charming,' said Roz.

'And Saul can go and screw himself,' had said Ian.

Saul waited until the two had gone off down the path to the sea, and said, 'Now, listen. I want to put it to you both. I want to get married again. As far as I'm concerned, Lil, you're the one. But you've got to decide.'

'It's no good,' said Roz, and Lil only shrugged. 'We can see how it must look. You're just about as good a bargain as any women look for.'

'And you're talking for Lil, again.'

'She's often enough spoken for herself.'

'But you'd both do better with a bloke,' he said. 'The two of you, without men, and the two lads. It's all too much of a good thing.'

A moment of shock. What was he saying? Implying?

But he was going on. 'You are two handsome girls,' said this gallant suitor. 'You're both so . . .' and then he seemed to freeze, his face showed he was struggling with emotions, violent ones, and then it set hard. He muttered, 'Oh, my God . . .' He stared at them, Lil to Roz and back again. 'My God,' he said again. 'You must think me a bloody fool.' His voice was toneless: the shock had gone deep.

'I'm an idiot,' he said. 'So, that's it.'

'What?' said Lil. 'What are you talking about?' Her voice was timid, because of what he might be talking about. Roz kicked her under the table. Lil actually leaned over to rub her ankle, still staring at Saul.

'A fool,' he said. 'You two must have been having a good laugh at my expense.' He got up and blundered out.

He was hardly able to get across the street to his own house.

'Oh, I see,' said Lil. She was about to go after him, but Roz said, 'Stop. It's a good thing, don't you see?'

'And now it's going to get around that we are lezzies,' said Lil.

'So what? Probably it wouldn't be the first time. After all, when you think how people talk.'

'I don't like it,' said Lil.

'Let them say it. The more the better. It keeps us all safe.'

Soon they all went to Saul's wedding with a handsome young woman who looked like Lil.

The two sons were pleased. But the women said to each other, 'We're neither of us likely to get as good a deal as Saul again.' That was Lil.

'No,' agreed Roz.

'And what are we going to do when the boys get tired of us old women?'

'I shall cry my eyes out. I shall go into a decline.'

'We shall grow old gracefully,' said Lil.

'Like hell,' said Roz. 'I shall fight every inch of the way.'

Not old women yet, nor anywhere near it. Over forty, though, and the boys were definitely not boys, and their time of wild beauty had gone. You'd not think now, see-ing the two strong, confident, handsome young men, that once they had drawn eyes struck as much by awe as by lust or love. And the two women, one day reminding themselves how their two had been like young gods, rummaged in old photographs, and could find nothing of what they knew had been there: just as, looking at their old photographs, they saw pretty girls, nothing more.

Ian was already working with his mother in the management of the chain of sports shops, and was an up-and-coming prominent citizen. Harder to make a mark in the theatre: Tom was still working in the foothills when Ian was already near the top. A new position for Tom, who had always been first, Ian looking up to him.

But he persevered. He worked. And as always he was charming with Lil, and as often in her bed as he could, considering the long and erratic hours of the theatre.

'There you are,' said Lil to Roz. 'It's a beginning. He's getting tired of me.'

But Ian showed no signs of relinquishing Roz, on the contrary. He was attentive, demanding, possessive, and when one day he saw her lying on her pillows, love-making just concluded, smoothing down loose ageing skin over her forearms, he let out a cry, clasped her, and shouted, 'No, don't, don't, don't even think of it. I won't let you grow old.'

'Well,' said Roz, 'it is going to happen, for all that.'

'No.' And he wept, just as he had done when he was still the frightened abandoned boy in her arms. 'No, Roz, please, I love you.'

'So I mustn't get old, is that it, Ian? I'm not allowed to? Mad, the boy is mad,' said Roz, addressing invisible listeners, as we do when sanity does not seem to have ears.

And alone, she felt uneasiness, and, indeed, awe. It was mad, his demand on her. It really did seem that he had refused to think she might grow old. Mad! But perhaps lunacy is one of the great invisible wheels that keep our world turning.

Meanwhile Tom's father had not given up his aim, to rescue Tom. He made no bones about it. 'I'm going to rescue you from those *femmes fatales*,' he said on the telephone. 'You get up here and let your old father take you in hand.'

'Harold is going to rescue me from you,' said Tom to his mother, on his way to Lil's bed. 'You're a bad influence.'

'A bit late,' said Roz.

Tom spent a fortnight in the university town. In the evenings a short walk took him out into the hot sandy scrub where hawks wheeled and watched. He became friends with Molly, Roz's successor, and with his half-sister, aged eight, and a new baby.

It was a boisterous child-centred house, but Tom told Ian he found it restful.

'Nice to get to know you, at last,' said Molly.

'And now,' said Harold, 'don't leave it so long.'

Tom didn't. He accepted an offer to direct *West Side Story* in the university theatre, and said he would stay in his father's house.

As always, the young women clustered and clung. 'Time you were married, your father thinks,' said Molly.

'Oh, does he?' said Tom. 'I'll marry in my own good time.'

He was in his late twenties. His classmates, his contemporaries, were married or had 'partners.'

There was a girl he did like, perhaps because of her difference from Lil and from Roz. She was a little dark-haired, ruddy-faced girl, pretty enough, and she flirted with him in a way that made no claims on him. For here, so far from home, from his mother and from Lil, he understood how many claims and ties bound him there. He admired his mother, even if she exasperated him, and he loved Lil. He could not imagine himself in bed with anyone else. But they bound him, oh, yes, they did, and Ian, too, a brother in reality if not in fact. Down there – so he apostrophised his city, his home, so much part of the sea that here, when he heard wind in the bushes it was the waves he heard. 'Down there, I'm not free.'

Up here, he was. He decided to accept work on another production. That meant another three months 'up here'. By now it was accepted that he and Mary Lloyd were a unit, 'an item'. Tom was passive, hearing this characterisation of him and Mary. He neither said yes, nor did he say no, he only laughed. But it was Mary who went with him to the cinema or who came home with him to his father for special meals.

'You could do a lot worse,' said Harold to his son.

'But I'm not doing anything, as far as I can see,' said Tom.

'Is that so? I don't think she sees it like that.'

Later Harold said to Tom, 'Mary asked me if you're queer?'

'Gay?' said Tom. 'Not as far as I know.'

It was breakfast time, the family ate at table, the girl watching what went on, as little girls do, the infant babbling attractively in her high chair. A delightful scene. Part of Tom ached for it, for his future, for himself. His father had wanted ordinary family life and here it was.

'Then, what gives?' asked Harold. 'Is there a girl back home, is that it?'

'You could say that,' said Tom, calmly helping himself to this and that.

'Then you should let Mary go,' said Harold.

'Yes,' said Molly, on behalf of her sex. 'It's not fair.'

'I wasn't aware I had her tied.'

'Tom,' said his father.

'That's not *on*,' said his father's wife.

Tom said nothing. Then he was in bed with Mary. He had slept only with Lil, no one else. This fresh young bouncy body was delightful, he liked it all, and took quiet satisfaction in Mary's, 'I thought you were gay, I really did.' Clearly, she was agreeably surprised.

So there it was. Mary came often to spend the night with Tom in Harold's and Molly's house, all very *en famille* and cosy. If weddings were not actually mentioned, that was because tact had been decided on. And because of something else, still ill-defined. In bed, Mary had exclaimed over the bite mark on Tom's calf. 'God,' said she. 'What was this? A dog?' 'That was a love bite,' he said, after thought. 'Who on earth . . .' And Mary, in play, tried to fit her mouth over the bite, but found Tom's leg, and then Tom, pulling away from her. 'Don't do that,' he said, which was fair enough. But then, in a voice she had certainly never heard from him, nor anything like it: 'Don't you dare ever do that again.'

She stared, and began to cry. He simply got off the bed and went off into the bathroom. He came back clothed, and did not look at her.

There was something here . . . something bad . . . some place where she must not go. Mary understood that. She felt so shocked by the incident that she nearly broke off from Tom, then and there.

Tom thought he might as well go back home. What he loved about being 'up here' was being free, and that delightful condition had evaporated.

This town was imprisoning him. It was not a large one, but that wasn't the point. He liked it, as a place, spreading suburbs of bungalows around a centre of university and business, and all around the scrubby shrubby desert. He could walk from the university theatre after rehearsal and find himself in ten minutes with strong-smelling thorny bushes all around, and under his feet coarse yellow sand where the fallen thorns made pale warning gleams: careful, don't tread on us, we can pierce through the thickest soles. At night, after a performance or a rehearsal, he walked straight out into the dark and stood listening to the crickets, and above him the unpolluted sky glittered and sparked off coloured fire. When he got back to his father's, Mary might be waiting for him.

'Where did you get to?'

'I went for a walk.'

'Why didn't you tell me? I like to walk too.'

'I'm a bit of a lone wolf,' said Tom. 'I'm the cat who walks by himself. So, if that's not your style, I'm sorry.'

'Hey,' said Mary. 'Don't bite my head off.'

'Well, you'd better know what you're letting yourself in for.'

At this, Harold and Molly exchanged glances: that was a commitment, surely? And Mary, hearing a promise, said 'I like cats. Luckily.'

But she was secretly tearful and fearful.

Tom was restless, he was moody. He was very unhappy but did not know it. He had not been unhappy in his life. He did not recognise the pain for what it was. There are people who are never ill, are unthinkingly healthy, then they get an illness and are so affronted and ashamed and afraid that they may even die of it. Tom was the emotional equivalent of such a person.

'What is it? What's wrong with me?' he groaned, waking with a heavy weight across his chest. 'I'd like to stay right here in bed and pull the covers over my head.'

But what for? There was nothing wrong with him.

Then, one evening, standing out under the stars, feeling sad enough to howl up at them, he said to himself, 'Good Lord, I'm so unhappy. Yes, that's it.'

He told Mary he wasn't well. When she was solicitous he said, 'Leave me alone.'

From the periphery of the little town, roads which soon became tracks ran out into the desert, to places used by students for their picnics and excursions. In between the used ways almost invisible paths made their way between the odoriferous bushes that had butterflies clinging to them in the day, and at night sent out waves of scent to attract bats. Tom walked out on the tarmacked road, turned on to the dusty track, turned off that and found a faint path to a little hill that had rocks on it, one a big flat one, which held the sun's heat well into the night. Tom lay on this hot rock and let unhappiness fill him.

'Lil,' he was whispering. 'Lil.'

He knew at last that he was missing Lil, that was the trouble. Why was he surprised? Vaguely, he had all this time thought that one day he'd get a girl his own age and then . . . but it had been so vague. Lil had always been in his life. He lay face down on the rock and sniffed at it, the faint metallic tang, the hot dust, and vegetable aromas from little plants in the cracks. He was thinking of Lil's body that always smelled of salt, of the sea. She was like a sea creature, in and out, the sea water often drying on her and then she was in again. He bit into his forearm, remembering that his earliest memory was of licking salt off Lil's shoulders. It was a game they played, the little boy and his mother's oldest friend. Every inch of his body had been available to Lil's strong hands since he had been born, and Lil's body was as familiar to him as his own. He saw again Lil's breasts, only just covered by the bikini top, and the faint wash of glistening sand in the cleft between her breasts, and the glitter of tiny sand grains on her shoulders.

'I used to lick her for the salt,' he murmured. 'Like an animal at a salt lick.'

When he went back, very late, the house dark, he did not sleep but sat down and wrote to Lil. Writing letters had not ever been his style. Finding his writing illegible, he remembered that an old portable typewriter had been stuffed under his bed, and he pulled it out, and typed, trying to muffle the sharp sound by putting the machine on a towel. But Molly had heard, knocked and said, 'Can't you sleep?' Tom said he was sorry, and stopped.

In the morning he finished the letter and posted it and wrote another. His father, peering to see the inscription, said, 'So, you're not writing to your mother?'

Tom said, 'No. As you see.' Family life had its drawbacks, he decided.

Thereafter he wrote letters to Lil at the university, and posted them himself.

Molly asked him what was the matter and he said he wasn't feeling up to scratch, and she said he should see a doctor.

Mary asked what was the matter and he said, 'I'm all right.'

And still he didn't go back 'down there'; he stayed up here, and that meant staying with Mary.

He wrote to Lil daily, answered the letters, or rather notes, she sometimes wrote to him; he telephoned his mother, he went out into the desert as often as he could, and told himself he would get over it. Not to worry.

Meanwhile his heart was a lump of cold loneliness, and he dreamed miserably.

'Listen,' said Mary, 'if you want to call this off, then say so.'

He suppressed, 'Call *what* off?' and said, 'Just give me time.'

Then, on an impulse, or perhaps because he soon would have to decide whether to accept another contract, he said to his father, 'I'm off.'

'What about Mary?' asked Molly.

He did not reply. Back home, he was over at Lil's and in her bed in an hour. But it was not the same. He could make comparisons now, and did. It was not that Lil was old – she was beautiful, so he kept muttering and whispering, 'You're so beautiful,' – but there was claim on him, Mary, and that wasn't even personal. Mary, another woman, did it matter? One day soon he must – he had to . . . everyone expected it of him.

Meanwhile Ian seemed to be doing fine with Roz. With his mother, Tom's. Ian didn't seem to be unhappy, or suffering, far from it.

And then Mary arrived, and found the four preparing to go to the sea. Flippers and goggles were found for her, and a surfboard. Within half an hour of her arrival she was ready to embark with the two young men, on the wide, dangerous, bad sea outside this safe bay. A little motorboat would take them out. So this pretty young thing, as smooth and shiny as a fish, larked about and played with Tom and Ian, and the two older women sat on their chairs, watching behind dark glasses and saw the motorboat arrive and take the three off.

'She's come for Tom,' said Tom's mother.

'Yes, I know,' said Tom's lover.

'She's nice enough,' said Roz.

Lil said nothing.

Roz said, 'Lil, I think this is where we bow out.'

Lil said nothing.

'Lil?' Roz peered over at her, and pushed up her dark glasses to see better.

'I don't think I could bear it,' said Lil.

'We've got to.'

'Ian doesn't have a girl.'

'No, but he should have. Lil, they're getting on towards thirty.'

'I know.'

Far away, where the sharp black rocks stood in their white foam at the mouth of the bay, three tiny figures were waving at them, before disappearing out of sight to the big beach.

'We have to stand together and end it,' said Roz.

Lil was quietly weeping. Then Roz was, too.

'We have to, Lil.'

'I know we do.'

'Come on, let's swim.'

The women swam hard and fast, out and back and around, and then landed on the beach, and went straight up to Roz's house, to prepare lunch. It was Sunday. Ahead was the long difficult afternoon.

Lil said, 'I've got work,' and went off to one of her shops.

Roz served lunch, making excuses for Lil, and then she too said she had things to do. Ian said he would come with her. That left Tom and Mary alone, and there was a showdown. 'Either on or off,' said Mary. 'Either yes or no.' 'There were plenty of fish in the sea.' 'It was time he grew up.' All that kind of thing, as prescribed for this occasion.

When the others came back, Mary announced that she and Tom were getting married, and there were congratulations and a noisy evening. Roz sang lots of songs, Tom joined in, they all sang. And when it was bedtime Mary stayed with Tom, in his house, and Ian went home with Lil.

Then Mary went back home to plan the wedding.

And now it had to be done. The two women said to the young men that now that was it. 'It's over,' said Roz.

Ian cried out, 'What do you mean? Why? I'm not getting married.'

Tom sat quietly, jaw set, drinking. He filled his glass with wine, drained it, filled it again, drank, saying nothing.

At last he said to Ian, 'They're right, don't you see?'

'No,' yelled Ian. He went into Roz's room and called her, and Tom went with Lil to her house. Ian wept and pleaded. 'Why, what for? We're perfectly happy. Why do you want to spoil it?' But Roz stuck it out. She was all heartless determination and only when she and Lil were alone together, the men having gone off to discuss it, they wept and said they could not bear it. Their hearts were breaking they said, how were they going to live, it would be unendurable.

When the men returned, the women were tear-stained but firm.

Lil told Tom that he must not come with her that night and Roz told Ian that he must go home with Lil.

'You've ruined everything,' said Ian to Roz. 'It's all your fault. Why couldn't you leave things as they were?'

Roz jested, 'Cheer up. We are going to become respectable ladies, yes, your disreputable mothers are going to become pillars of virtue. We shall be perfect mothers-in-law, and then we shall become wonderful grandmothers to your children.'

'I'm not going to forgive you,' said Ian to Roz.

And Tom said to Lil, low, to her only, 'I'll never ever ever forget you.'

Now, that was a valediction, almost conventional. It meant – surely? – that Tom's heart was not likely to suffer permanent damage.

The wedding, needless to say, was a grand affair. Mary had been determined not to be upstaged by her dramatic mother-in-law, but found Roz was being the soul of tact, in a self-effacing outfit. Lil was elegant and pale and smiling, and the very moment the happy pair had driven off for their honeymoon she was down swimming in the bay, where Roz, a good hostess, could not leave her guests to join her. Later Roz crossed the street to find out how Lil was, but her bedroom door was locked and she would not respond to Roz's knocks and enquiries. Ian as best man had made a funny and likeable speech, and, meeting Roz in the street as she was returning from Lil's, said, 'So? Are you pleased with yourself now?' And he too went running down to the sea.

Now Roz was in her empty house, and she lay on her bed and at last was able to weep. When there were knocks at her door which she knew were Ian's, she rolled in anguish, her fist stuffed into her mouth.

As soon as the honeymoon was over, Mary told Tom, who told his mother, that she thought Roz should move out and leave the house to them. It made sense. It was a big house, right for a family. The trouble was financial. Years ago the house had been affordable, when this whole area had been far from desirable, but now it was smart and only the rich could afford these houses. In an impulsive, reckless, generous gesture, Roz gave the house to the young couple as a wedding present. And so where was she to live? She couldn't afford another house like this. She took up residence in a little hotel down the coast, and this meant that, for the first time ever, since she was born, she was not within a few yards of Lil. She did not understand at first why she was so restless, sad, bereft, put it all down to losing Ian, but then understood it was Lil she missed, almost as much as Ian. She felt she had lost everything, and literally from one week to the next. But she was not reflective, by nature: she was like Tom, who would always be surprised by his emotions, when he was forced to notice them. To deal with her feelings of emptiness and loss, she accepted a job at the university as a full-time teacher of drama, worked hard, swam twice a day, took sleeping pills.

Mary was soon pregnant. Jokes of a traditional kind were aimed at Ian, by Saul, among others. 'You aren't going to let your mate get ahead of you, are you? When's your wedding?'

Ian was working hard, too. He was trying not to give himself time to think. No stranger to thought, reflection, introspection, he felt that they were enemies, waiting to strike him down. A new shop was opening in the town where Harold was. They were waiting for their child. Ian did not stay at Harold's, but in a hotel, and of course visited Harold, who had been like a father to him – so he said. There he met a friend of Mary's, who had paid attention to him at the wedding. Hannah. It was not that he disliked her, on the contrary, she pleased him, with her comfortable ways, that were easy to see as maternal, but he was inside an empty space full of echoes, and he could not imagine making love with anyone but Roz. He swam every morning from 'their' beach, sometimes seeing Roz there, and he greeted her, but turned away, as if the sight of her hurt him – it did. And he more often took the little motorboat out to the surfing beaches. He and Tom had always gone together, but Tom was so busy with Mary, and the new baby.

One day, seeing Roz drying herself on the sand, the boatman, who had come into the bay especially to find her, stopped his engine, let the boat rock on the gentle waves, and jumped down into the water, tugging the boat behind him like a dog on a leash to say, 'Mrs Struthers, Ian's doing some pretty dangerous stuff out there. He's a picture to watch, but he scares me. If you see his mother – or perhaps you . . .'

Roz said, 'Well, now. To tell a man like Ian to play it safe, that's more than a mother's life is worth. Or mine, for that matter.'

'Someone should warn him. He's asking for it. Those waves out there, you've got to respect them.'

'Have you warned him?'

'I've tried my best.'

'Thanks,' said Roz. 'I'll tell his mother.'

She told Lil, who said to her son that he was playing too close to the safety margins. If the old boatman was worried, then that meant something. Ian said, 'Thanks.'

One evening, at sunset, the boatman came in to find Roz or one of them on the beach, but had to go up to the house, found Mary, told her that Ian was lying smashed up on one of the outer beaches.

Then Ian was in hospital. Told by the doctor, 'You'll live,' his face said plainly he wished he could have heard something else. He had hurt his spine. But that would probably heal. He had hurt his leg, and that would never be normal.

He left hospital and lay in his bed at home, in a room

which for years had not been much more than a place where he changed his clothes, before crossing the street to Roz. But in that house were now Tom and Mary. He turned his face to the wall. His mother tried to coax him up and on to his feet, but could not make him take exercise. Lil could not, but Hannah could and did. She came to visit her old friend Mary, slept in that house, and spent most of her time sitting with Ian, holding his hand, often in sympathetic tears.

'For an athlete it must be so hard,' she kept saying to Lil, to Mary, to Tom. 'I can understand why he is so discouraged.'

A good word, an accurate one. She persuaded Ian to turn his face towards her, and then, soon, to get up and take the prescribed steps up and down the room, then on to the verandah, and soon, across the road and down to swim. But he would not ever surf again. He would always limp.

Hannah kissed the poor leg, kissed him, and Ian wept with her: her tears gave him permission to weep. And soon there was another wedding, an even larger one, since Ian and his mother Liliane were so well known, and their sports shops so beneficial to every town they found themselves in, and both were famed for their good causes and their general benevolence.

So there they were, the new young couple, Ian and Hannah, in Lil's house with Lil. Opposite, Roz's old house was now Tom's and Mary's. Lil was uncomfortable in her role as mother-in-law, and was unhappy every time she saw the house opposite, now so changed. But after all, she was rich, unlike Roz. She bought one of the houses almost on the beach, not a couple of hundred yards from the two young couples, and Roz moved in. The women were together again, and Saul Butler when he met them allowed a special measure of sarcastic comment into his, 'Ah, together again, I see!' 'As you see,' said Roz or Lil. 'Can't fool you, Saul, can we?' said Lil, or Roz.

Then Hannah was pregnant and Ian was appropriately proud.

'It has turned out all right,' said Roz to Lil.

'Yes, I suppose so,' said Lil.

'What more could we expect?'

They were on the beach, in their old chairs, moved to outside the new fence.

'I didn't expect anything,' said Lil.

'But?'

'I didn't expect to feel the way I do,' said Lil. 'I feel . . .'

'All right,' said Roz quickly. 'Let it go. I know. But look at it this way, we've had . . .'

'The best,' said Lil. 'Now all that time seems to me like a dream. I can't believe it, such happiness, Roz,' she whispered, turning her face and leaning forward a little, though there wasn't a soul for fifty yards.

'I know,' said Roz. 'Well – that's it.' And she leaned back, shutting her eyes. From below her dark glasses tears trickled.

Ian went off with his mother a good bit on trips to their shops. He was everywhere greeted with affectionate, respectful generosity. It was known how he had got his limp. As foolhardy as an Everest hero, as brave as – well, as a man outrunning a wave like a mountain – he was so handsome, so courteous, such a gentleman, so kind. He was like his mother.

On one such trip, they were in their hotel suite, before bedtime, and Lil was saying that she was going to take little Alice for the day when she got back to give Mary a chance to go shopping.

Ian said, 'You two women are really pleased with yourselves.'

This was venomous, not like him; she had not – she thought – heard that voice from him before.

'Yes,' he said, 'it's all right for you.'

'What do you mean, Ian, what are you saying?'

'I'm not blaming you. I know it was Roz.'

'What do you mean? It was both of us.'

'Roz put the idea into your head. I know that. You'd never have thought of it. Too bad about Tom. Too bad about me.'

At this she began to laugh, a weak defensive laugh. She was thinking of the years with Tom, watching him change from a beautiful boy into a man, seeing the years claim him, knowing how it must end, must end, then should end, she should end it . . . she and Roz . . . but it was so hard, hard . . .

'Ian, do you realise, you sound demented when you say things like that?'

'Why? I don't see it.'

'What did you think? We'd all just go on, indefinitely, then you and Tom, two middle-aged men, bachelors, and Roz and me, old and then you two, old, without families, and Roz and I, old, old, old . . . we're getting on for old now, can't you see?'

'No, you aren't,' said her son calmly. 'Not at all. You and Roz knock the girls for six any time.'

Did he mean Hannah and Mary? If so . . . the streak here of sheer twisted lunacy frightened her and she got up. 'I'm going to bed.'

'It was Roz put you up to it. I don't forgive you for agreeing. And she needn't think I'll forgive her for spoiling everything. We were all so happy.'

'Good night, I'll see you at breakfast.'

Hannah had her baby, Shirley, and the two young women were much together. The two older women, and the husbands, waited to hear news of second pregnancies: surely the logical step. And then, to their surprise, Mary and Hannah announced that they thought of going into business together. At once it was suggested they should work in the sports shops: they would have flexible hours, could come and go, earn a bit of money . . . And, it was the corollary, fit second babies into a comfortable time-table.

They said no, they wanted to start a new business, the two of them.

'I expect we can help you with the money,' said Ian, and Hannah said, 'No, thanks. Mary's father can help us out. He's loaded.' When Hannah spoke, it was often Mary's thought they were hearing. 'We want to be independent,' said Hannah, a trifle apologetic, herself hearing that she had sounded ungracious, to say the least.

The wives went off to visit their families for a weekend, taking the babies, to show them off.

The four, Lil and Roz, Ian and Tom, sat together at the table in Roz's house – Roz's former house – and the sound of the waves said that nothing had changed, nothing . . . except that the infant Alice's paraphernalia was all over the place, in the way of modern family life.

'It's very odd, what they want,' said Roz. 'Do we understand why? What is it all about?'

'We're too – heavy for them,' said Lil.

'We. They,' said Ian. 'They. We.'

They all looked at him, to take in what he meant.

Then Roz burst out, 'We've tried so hard. Lil and I, we've done our best.'

'I know you have,' said Tom. 'We know that.'

'But here we are,' said Ian. 'Here *we* are.'

And now he leaned forwards towards Roz, passionate, accusing – very far from the urbane and affable man everyone knew: 'And nothing has changed, has it. Roz? Just tell me the truth, tell me, has it?'

Roz's eyes, full of tears, did meet his, and then she got up to save herself with the ritual of supplying cold drinks from the fridge.

Lil said, looking calmly straight across at Tom, 'It's no

good, Roz. Just don't, don't . . .' For Roz was crying, silently, allowing it to be seen, her dark glasses lying on the table. Then she covered her eyes with the glasses, and directing those dark circles at Ian, she said, 'I don't understand what it is you want, Ian. Why do you go on and on? It's all done. It's finished.'

'So, you don't understand,' said Ian.

'Stop it,' said Lil, beginning to cry, too. 'What's the point of this? All we have to do is to decide what to tell them, they want our support.'

'*We* will tell *them* that *we* will support *them*,' said Ian, and added, 'I'm going for a swim.'

And the four ran down into the waves, Ian limping, but not too badly.

Interesting that in the discussion that afternoon, with the four, a certain key question had not been mentioned. If the two young wives were going to start a business, then the grandmothers would have to play a part.

A second discussion, with all six of them, was on this very point.

'Working grandmothers,' said Roz. 'I quite fancy it, what about you, Lil?'

'Working is the word,' said Lil. 'I'm not going to give up the shops. How will we fit in the babies?'

'Easy,' said Roz. 'We'll juggle it. I have long holidays at the university. You have Ian at your beck and call in the shops. There are weekends. And I daresay the girls'll want to see their little angels from time to time.'

'You're not suggesting we're going to neglect them?' said Mary.

'No, darling, no, not at all. Besides, both Lil and I had girls to help us with our little treasures, didn't we, Lil?'

'I suppose so. Not much, though.'

'Oh, well,' said Mary, 'I suppose we can hire an *au pair*, if it's like that.'

'How you do flare up,' said Roz. 'Certainly we can get ourselves *au pairs* when needed. Meanwhile, the grannies are at your service.'

It was a real ritual occasion, the day the babies were to be introduced to the sea. All six adults were there on the beach. Blankets had been spread. The grandmothers, Roz and Lil, in their bikinis, were sitting with the babies between their knees, smoothing them over with suncream. Tiny, delicate creatures, fair-haired, fair-skinned, and around them, tall and large and protective, the big adults.

The mummies took them into the sea, assisted by Tom and Lil. There was much splashing, cries of fear and delight from the little ones, reassurance from the adults – a noisy scene. And sitting on the blankets where the sand had already blown, glistening in little drifts, were Roz and Ian. Ian looked long and intently at Roz and said, 'Take your glasses off.' Roz did so.

He said, 'I don't like it when you hide your eyes from me.'

She snapped the glasses back on and said, 'Stop it, Ian. You've got to stop this. It's simply not *on*.'

He was reaching forward to lift off her glasses. She slapped down his hand. Lil had seen, from where she stood to her waist in the sea. The intensity of it, you could say, even the ferocity . . . had Hannah noticed? Had Mary? A yell from a little girl – Alice. A big wave had leaped up and . . . 'It's bitten me,' she shrieked. 'The sea's bitten me.' Up jumped Ian, reached Shirley who also was making a commotion now. 'Can't you see,' he shouted at Hannah, over the sea noise, 'you're frightening her? They're frightened.' With a tiny child on either shoulder he limped up out of the waves. He began a jiggling and joggling of the little girls in a kind of dance, but he was dipping in each step with the limp and they began to cry harder. 'Granny,' wailed Hannah, 'I want my granny,' sobbed Shirley. The infants were deposited on the rugs, Lil joined Roz, and the grandmothers soothed and petted the children while the other four went off to swim.

'There, my ducky,' sang Roz, to Hannah.

'Poor little pet,' crooned Lil to Shirley.

Not long after this the two young women were in their new office, in the suite which would be the scene of their – they were convinced – future triumphs. 'We are having a little celebration,' they had said, making it sound as if there would be associates, sponsors, friends. But they were alone, drinking champagne and already tiddly.

It was the end of their first year. They had worked hard, harder than they had expected. Things had gone so well there was already talk of expanding. That would mean even longer hours, and more work for the grandmothers.

'They wouldn't mind,' said Hannah.

'I think they would,' said Mary.

There was something in her voice, and Hannah looked to see what Mary was wanting her to understand. Then, she said, 'It's not a question of us working our butts off – and their working their butts off – they want us to get pregnant again.'

'Exactly,' said Mary.

'I wouldn't mind,' said Hannah. 'I told Ian, yes, but there's no hurry. We can get our business established and then let's see. But you're right, that's what they want.'

'They,' said Mary. '*They* want. And what *they* want they intend to have.'

Here Hannah showed signs of unrest. Compliant by nature, biddable, she had begun by deferring to Mary, such a strong character, but now she was asserting herself. 'I think they are very kind.'

'They,' said Mary. 'Who the hell are *they* to be kind to *us*?'

'Oh, come on! We wouldn't have been able to start this business at all without the grandmothers helping with everything.'

'Roz is so damned tactful all the time,' said Mary, and it exploded out of her, the champagne aiding and abetting. She poured some more. 'They're both so tactful.'

'You must be short of something to complain about.'

'I feel they are watching us all the time to make sure we come up to the mark.'

'What mark?'

'I don't know,' said Mary, tears imminent. 'I wish I knew. There's something *there*.'

'They don't want to be interfering mothers-in-law.'

'Sometimes I hate them.'

'*Hate*,' Hannah dismissed, with a smile.

'They've got them, don't you see? Sometimes I feel . . .'

'It's because they didn't have fathers – the boys. Ian's father died and Tom's went off and married someone else. That's why the four of them are so close.'

'I don't care why. Sometimes I feel like a spare part.'

'I think you're being unfair.'

'Tom wouldn't care who he was married to. It could be a seagull or a . . . or a . . . wombat.'

Hannah flung herself back in her chair, laughing.

'I mean it. Oh, he's ever so damned kind. He's so nice. I shout at him and I pick a fight, anything just to make him – see me. And then the next thing we're in bed having a good screw.'

But Hannah didn't feel anything like that. She knew Ian needed her. It was not only the slight dependence because of his gammy leg, he sometimes clung to her, childlike. Yes, there was something of the child in him – a little. One night he had called out to Roz in his sleep, and Hannah had woken him. 'You were dreaming of Roz,' she told him.

At once awake and wary, he said, 'Hardly surprising. I've known her all my life. She was like another mother.' And he buried his face in her breasts. 'Oh, Hannah, I don't know what I'd do without you.'

Now that Hannah was standing up to her, Mary was even more alone. Once she had felt, there's Hannah, at least I've got Hannah.

Thinking over this conversation afterwards, Mary knew there was something there that eluded her. That was what she always felt. And yet what was she complaining about? Hannah was right. When she looked at their situation from outside, married to these two covetable men, well-known, well-set-up, well-off, generally liked – so what was she complaining about? I have everything, she decided. But then, a voice from her depths – I have nothing. She lacked everything. 'I have nothing,' she told herself, as waves of emptiness swept over her. In the deep centre of her life – nothing, an absence.

And yet she could not put her finger on it, what was wrong, what was lacking. So there must be something wrong with her. She, Mary, was at fault. But why? What was it? So she puzzled, sometimes so unhappy she felt she could run away out of the situation for good.

When Mary found the bundle of letters, forgotten in an old bit of luggage, she had at first thought they were all from Lil to Tom, conventional, of the kind you'd ex-pect from an old friend or even a second mother. They began, Dear Tom and ended Love, Lil, with sometimes a cross or two for a kiss. And then there was the other letter, from Tom to Lil, that had not been posted. 'Why shouldn't I write to you, Lil, why not, I have to, I think of you all the time, oh my God, Lil, I love you so much, I dream of you, I can't bear being apart from you, I love you I love you . . .' and so on, pages of it. So, she read Lil's letters again, and saw them differently. And then she understood everything. And when she stood on the path with Hannah, below Baxter's Gardens, and heard Roz's laughter, she knew it was mocking laughter. It mocked her, Mary, and she understood everything at last. It was all clear to her.

About the author

About the book

Read on

Insights,
Interviews
& More...

Meet Doris Lessing

© Ingrid von Kruse

DORIS LESSING was born Doris May Tayler in Persia (now Iran) on October 22, 1919. Both of her parents were British: her father, who had been crippled in World War I, was a clerk in the Imperial Bank of Persia; her mother had been a nurse. In 1925, lured by the promise of getting rich through maize farming, the family moved to the British colony of Southern Rhodesia (now Zimbabwe). Doris's mother adapted to the rough life of the settlement, energetically trying to reproduce what was, in her view, a "civilized" Edwardian life among "savages," but her father did not, and

❝ Lessing has described her childhood as an uneven mix of some pleasure and much pain. ❞

the thousand-odd acres of bush he had bought failed to yield the promised wealth.

Lessing has described her childhood as an uneven mix of some pleasure and much pain. The natural world, which she explored with her brother, Harry, was one retreat from an otherwise miserable existence. Her mother, obsessed with raising a proper daughter, enforced a rigid system of rules and hygiene at home and then installed Doris in a convent school, where the nuns terrified their charges with stories of hell and damnation. Lessing was later sent to Salisbury, the capital of Southern Rhodesia, where she briefly attended an all-girls high school before dropping out. She was thirteen, and it was the end of her formal education.

But like other women writers from southern Africa who did not graduate from high school, such as Olive Schreiner and Nadine Gordimer, Lessing made herself into a self-educated intellectual. She once commented that unhappy childhoods seem to produce fiction writers: "Yes, I think that is true. Though it wasn't apparent to me then. Of course, I wasn't thinking in terms of being a writer then— I was just thinking about how to escape, all the time." The parcels of books ordered from London fed her imagination, laying out other worlds to escape into. Lessing's early reading included Dickens, Scott, Stevenson, and Kipling; later she discovered D. H. Lawrence, Stendhal, Tolstoy, and Dostoyevsky. Bedtime stories also nurtured her youth; her mother told them to the children, and Doris herself kept her younger brother awake, spinning out tales. Doris's formative years were also spent absorbing her father's bitter memories of World War I, taking them in as a kind of "poison." "We are all of us made by war," Lessing has written, "twisted and warped by war, but we seem to forget it."

In flight from her mother, Lessing left home when she was fifteen and took a job as a nursemaid. Her employer gave her books on politics and sociology to read, while his brother-in-law crept into her bed at night and gave her inept kisses. During that time she was, Lessing has written, "in a fever of erotic longing." Frustrated by her backward suitor, she indulged in elaborate romantic fantasies. She was also writing stories, and sold two to magazines in South Africa.

Lessing's life has been a challenge to her belief that people cannot resist the currents of their time, as she fought against biological and cultural imperatives that fated her to sink without a murmur into marriage and motherhood. "There is a whole generation of ▶

women," she has said, speaking of her mother's era, "and it was as if their lives came to a stop when they had children. Most of them got pretty neurotic—because, I think, of the contrast between what they were taught at school they were capable of being and what actually happened to them." Lessing believes that she was freer than most people because she became a writer. For her, writing is a process of "setting at a distance," taking "the raw, the individual, the uncriticized, the unexamined, into the realm of the general."

In 1937 she moved to Salisbury, where she worked as a telephone operator for a year. At nineteen she married Frank Wisdom, with whom she had two children. A few years later, feeling trapped in a persona that she feared would destroy her, she left her family, remaining in Salisbury. Soon she was drawn to the like-minded members of the Left Book Club, a group of Communists "who read everything, and who did not think it remarkable to read." Gottfried Lessing was a central member of the group; shortly after she joined, they married and had a son.

During the postwar years, Lessing became increasingly disillusioned with the Communist movement, which she left altogether in 1954. By 1949, Lessing had moved to London with her young son. That year, she also published her first novel, *The Grass Is Singing*, and began her career as a professional writer.

Lessing's fiction is deeply autobiographical, much of it emerging out of her experiences in Africa. Drawing upon her childhood memories and her serious engagement with politics and social concerns, Lessing has written about the clash of cultures, the gross injustices of racial inequality, the struggle among opposing elements within an individual's own personality, and the conflict between the individual conscience and the collective good. Her stories and novellas set in Africa, published during the fifties and early sixties, decry the dispossession of black Africans by white colonials and expose the sterility of the white culture in southern Africa. In 1956, in response to Lessing's outrageous outspokenness, she was declared a prohibited alien in both Southern Rhodesia and South Africa.

Over the years, Lessing has attempted to accommodate what she admires in the novels of the nineteenth century—their "climate of ethical judgment"—to the demands of twentieth-century ideas about consciousness and time. After writing the Children of Violence series (1952–1959), a formally conventional *bildungsroman* (novel of education) about the growth in consciousness of its heroine, Martha Quest, Lessing broke new ground with *The Golden Notebook* (1962). This novel was a daring narrative experiment, in which the multiple selves of a contemporary woman are rendered in astonishing depth and detail. Anna Wulf, like Lessing herself, strives for ruthless honesty as she aims to free herself from the chaos, emotional numbness, and hypocrisy afflicting her generation.

Attacked for being "unfeminine" in her depiction of female anger and aggression, Lessing responded, "Apparently what many women were thinking, feeling, experiencing came as a great surprise." As at least one critic noticed, Anna Wulf "tries to live with the freedom of a man," a point Lessing seems to confirm: "These attitudes in male writers were taken for granted, accepted as sound philosophical bases, as quite normal, certainly not as woman-hating, aggressive, or neurotic."

In the 1970s and 1980s, Lessing began to explore more fully the quasi-mystical insight Anna Wulf seems to reach by the end of *The Golden Notebook*. Her "inner-space fiction" deals with cosmic fantasies (*Briefing for a Descent into Hell*, 1971), dreamscapes and other dimensions (*Memoirs of a Survivor*, 1974), and science fiction probings of higher planes of existence (the series Canopus in Argos: Archives, 1979–1983). These reflect Lessing's interest, since the 1960s, in Idries Shah, whose writings on Sufi mysticism stress the evolution of consciousness and the belief that individual liberation can come about only if people understand the link between their own fates and the fate of society.

Lessing's other works include *The Good Terrorist* (1985) and *The Fifth Child* (1988); she also published two novels under the pseudonym Jane Somers (*The Diary of a Good Neighbor*, 1983, and *If the Old Could . . .* , 1984). In addition, she has written several nonfiction works, including books about cats, a love since childhood. In the last decade of the twentieth century, Lessing published a variety of books, including *The Real Thing* (stories, 1992); *African Laughter* (reportage, 1992); two volumes of autobiography, *Under My Skin* (1994) and *Walking in the Shade* (1997); and the novel *Mara and Dann: An Adventure* (1999). ▶

Ben, in the World, the poignant sequel to *The Fifth Child*, was published in 2000, followed by the novels *The Sweetest Dream* (2002), *The Grandmothers: Four Short Novels* (2003), *The Story of General Dann and Mara's Daughter, Griot and the Snow Dog* (2006, sequel to *Mara and Dann*), and *The Cleft* (2007). In 2008 she published *Alfred & Emily*, an exploration of the lives of her parents through both fiction and memoir.

In 2007, Lessing was awarded the Nobel Prize in Literature. ∽

On Not Winning the Nobel Prize
The Nobel Lecture

Doris Lessing was awarded the Nobel Prize in 2007. Owing to back problems, she was unable to deliver her lecture in person. The lecture was delivered by her British publisher, Nicholas Pearson, at the Swedish Academy, Stockholm, on December 7, 2007.

I AM STANDING in a doorway looking through clouds of blowing dust to where I am told there is still uncut forest. Yesterday I drove through miles of stumps and charred remains of fires where, in '56, there was the most wonderful forest I have ever seen, all now destroyed. People have to eat. They have to get fuel for fires.

This is northwest Zimbabwe in the early eighties, and I am visiting a friend who was a teacher in a school in London. He is here "to help Africa," as we put it. He is a gently idealistic soul, and what he found in this school shocked him into a depression, from which it was hard to recover. This school is like every other built after Independence. It consists of four large brick rooms side by side, put straight into the dust, one two three four, with a half room at one end, which is the library. In these classrooms are blackboards, but my friend keeps the chalks in his pocket, as otherwise they would be stolen. There is no atlas or globe in the school, no textbooks, no exercise books or biros. In the library there are no books of the kind the pupils would like to read, but only tomes from American ▶

universities, hard even to lift, rejects from white libraries, or novels with titles like *Weekend in Paris* and *Felicity Finds Love.*

There is a goat trying to find sustenance in some aged grass. The headmaster has embezzled the school funds and is suspended, arousing the question familiar to all of us but usually in more august contexts: How is it these people behave like this when they must know everyone is watching them?

My friend doesn't have any money because everyone, pupils and teachers, borrow from him when he is paid and will probably never pay him back. The pupils range from six to twenty-six, because some who did not get schooling as children are here to make it up. Some pupils walk many miles every morning, rain or shine and across rivers. They cannot do homework because there is no electricity in the villages, and you can't study easily by the light of a burning log. The girls have to fetch water and cook before they set off for school and when they get back.

As I sit with my friend in his room, people drop in shyly, and everyone begs for books. "Please send us books when you get back to London," one man says. "They taught us to read but we have no books." Everybody I met, everyone, begged for books.

I was there some days. The dust blew. The pumps had broken and the women were having to fetch water from the river. Another idealistic teacher from England was rather ill after seeing what this "school" was like.

On the last day they slaughtered the goat. They cut it into bits and cooked it in a great tin. This was the much anticipated end-of-term feast: boiled goat and porridge. I drove away while it was still going on, back through the charred remains and stumps of the forest.

I do not think many of the pupils of this school will get prizes.

The next day I am to give a talk at a school in North London, a very good school, whose name we all know. It is a school for boys, with beautiful buildings and gardens.

These children here have a visit from some well-known person every week, and it is in the nature of things that these may be fathers, relatives, even mothers of the pupils. A visit from a celebrity is not unusual for them.

As I talk to them, the school in the blowing dust of northwest

Zimbabwe is in my mind, and I look at the mildly expectant English faces in front of me and try to tell them about what I have seen in the last week. Classrooms without books, without textbooks, or an atlas, or even a map pinned to a wall. A school where the teachers beg to be sent books to tell them how to teach, they being only eighteen or nineteen themselves. I tell these English boys how everybody begs for books: "Please send us books." I am sure that anyone who has ever given a speech will know that moment when the faces you are looking at are blank. Your listeners cannot hear what you are saying; there are no images in their minds to match what you are telling them—in this case the story of a school standing in dust clouds, where water is short, and where the end-of-term treat is a just-killed goat cooked in a great pot.

Is it really so impossible for these privileged students to imagine such bare poverty?

I do my best. They are polite.

I'm sure that some of them will one day win prizes.

Then, the talk is over. Afterwards I ask the teachers how the library is, and if the pupils read. In this privileged school, I hear what I always hear when I go to such schools and even universities.

"You know how it is," one of the teachers says. "A lot of the boys have never read at all, and the library is only half used."

Yes, indeed we do know how it is. All of us.

We are in a fragmenting culture, where our certainties of even a few decades ago are questioned and where it is common for young men and women, who have had years of education, to know nothing of the world, to have read nothing, knowing only some speciality or other, for instance, computers.

What has happened to us is an amazing invention—computers and the Internet and TV. It is a revolution. This is not the first revolution the human race has dealt with. The printing revolution, which did not take place in a matter of a few decades, but took much longer, transformed our minds and ways of thinking. A foolhardy lot, we accepted it all, as we always do, never asked, What is going to happen to us now, with this invention of print? In the same way, we never thought to ask, How will our lives, our way of thinking, be changed by this Internet, which has seduced a whole generation with its inanities so that even quite reasonable people ▶

will confess that once they are hooked, it is hard to cut free, and they may find a whole day has passed in blogging, etc.

Very recently, anyone even mildly educated would respect learning, education, and our great store of literature. Of course, we all know that when this happy state was with us, people would pretend to read, would pretend respect for learning. But it is on record that working men and women longed for books, and this is evidenced by the founding of working men's libraries and institutes, the colleges of the eighteenth and nineteenth centuries.

Reading, books, used to be part of a general education.

Older people, talking to young ones, must understand just how much of an education reading was, because the young ones know so much less. And if children cannot read, it is because they have not read.

We all know this sad story.

But we do not know the end of it.

We think of the old adage, "Reading maketh a full man"—and forgetting about jokes to do with overeating—reading makes a woman and a man full of information, of history, of all kinds of knowledge.

But we in the West are not the only people in the world. Not long ago, a friend who had been in Zimbabwe told me about a village where people had not eaten for three days but they were still talking about books and how to get them, about education.

I belong to an organization which started out with the intention of getting books into the villages. There was a group of people who in another connection had traveled Zimbabwe at its grass roots. They told me that the villages, unlike what is reported, are full of intelligent people, teachers retired, teachers on leave, children on holidays, old people. I myself paid for a little survey to discover what people in Zimbabwe want to read, and found the results were the same as those of a Swedish survey I had not known about. People want to read the same kinds of books that we in Europe want to read—novels of all kinds, science fiction, poetry, detective stories, plays, and do-it-yourself books, like how to open a bank account. All of Shakespeare too. A problem with finding books for villagers is that they don't know what is available, so a set book, like *The Mayor of Casterbridge*, becomes popular simply because it just happens to be there. *Animal Farm*, for obvious reasons, is the most popular of all novels.

Our organization was helped from the very start by Norway, and then by Sweden. Without this kind of support our supplies of books would have dried up. We got books from wherever we could. Remember, a good paperback from England costs a month's wages in Zimbabwe: that was *before* Mugabe's reign of terror. Now with inflation, it would cost several years' wages. But having taken a box of books out to a village—and remember there is a terrible shortage of petrol—I can tell you that the box was greeted with tears. The library may be a plank on bricks under a tree. And within a week there will be literacy classes—people who can read teaching those who can't, citizenship classes—and in one remote village, since there were no novels written in the language Tonga, a couple of lads sat down to write novels in Tonga. There are six or so main languages in Zimbabwe and there are novels in all of them: violent, incestuous, full of crime and murder.

It is said that a people gets the government it deserves, but I do not think it is true of Zimbabwe. And we must remember that this respect and hunger for books comes not from Mugabe's regime, but from the one before it, the whites. It is an astonishing phenomenon, this hunger for books, and it can be seen everywhere from Kenya down to the Cape of Good Hope.

This links improbably with a fact: I was brought up in what was virtually a mud hut, thatched. This kind of house has been built always, everywhere there are reeds or grass, suitable mud, poles for walls. Saxon England for example. The one I was brought up in had four rooms, one beside another, and it was full of books. Not only did my parents take books from England to Africa, but my mother ordered books by post from England for her children. Books arrived in great brown paper parcels, and they were the joy of my young life. A mud hut, but full of books.

Even today I get letters from people living in a village that might not have electricity or running water, just like our family in our elongated mud hut. "I shall be a writer too," they say, "because I've the same kind of house you lived in."

But here is the difficulty, no?

Writing, writers, do not come out of houses without books. ▸

There is the gap. There is the difficulty.

I have been looking at the speeches by some of your recent prizewinners. Take the magnificent Pamuk. He said his father had five hundred books. His talent did not come out of the air, he was connected with the great tradition.

Take V. S. Naipaul. He mentions that the Indian Vedas were close behind the memory of his family. His father encouraged him to write, and when he got to England he would visit the British Library. So he was close to the great tradition.

Let us take John Coetzee. He was not only close to the great tradition, he was the tradition: he taught literature in Cape Town. And how sorry I am that I was never in one of his classes, taught by that wonderfully brave, bold mind.

In order to write, in order to make literature, there must be a close connection with libraries, books, with the Tradition.

I have a friend from Zimbabwe, a black writer. He taught himself to read from the labels on jam jars, the labels on preserved fruit cans. He was brought up in an area I have driven through, an area for rural blacks. The earth is grit and gravel; there are low sparse bushes. The huts are poor, nothing like the well-cared-for huts of the better off. A school—but like one I have described. He found a discarded children's encyclopedia on a rubbish heap and taught himself from that.

On Independence in 1980 there was a group of good writers in Zimbabwe, truly a nest of singing birds. They were bred in old Southern Rhodesia, under the whites—the mission schools, the better schools. Writers are not made in Zimbabwe. Not easily, not under Mugabe.

All the writers traveled a difficult road to literacy, let alone to becoming writers. I would say learning to read from the printed labels on jam jars and discarded encyclopedias was not uncommon. And we are talking about people hungering for standards of education beyond them, living in huts with many children— an overworked mother, a fight for food and clothing.

Yet despite these difficulties, writers came into being. And we should also remember that this was Zimbabwe, conquered less than a hundred years before. The grandparents of these people might have been storytellers working in the oral tradition. In one or two generations there was the transition from stories remembered and passed on, to print, to books. What an achievement.

Books, literally wrested from rubbish heaps and the detritus of the white man's world. But a sheaf of paper is one thing, a published book quite another. I have had several accounts sent to me of the publishing scene in Africa. Even in more privileged places like North Africa, with its different tradition, to talk of a publishing scene is a dream of possibilities.

Here I am talking about books never written, writers that could not make it because the publishers are not there. Voices unheard. It is not possible to estimate this great waste of talent, of potential. But even before that stage of a book's creation which demands a publisher, an advance, encouragement, there is something else lacking.

Writers are often asked, How do you write? With a word processor? an electric typewriter? a quill? longhand? But the essential question is, Have you found a space, that empty space, which should surround you when you write? Into that space, which is like a form of listening, of attention, will come the words, the words your characters will speak, ideas—inspiration.

If a writer cannot find this space, then poems and stories may be stillborn.

When writers talk to each other, what they discuss is always to do with this imaginative space, this other time. "Have you found it? Are you holding it fast?"

Let us now jump to an apparently very different scene. We are in London, one of the big cities. There is a new writer. We cynically enquire, Is she good-looking? If this is a man, charismatic? Handsome? We joke but it is not a joke.

This new find is acclaimed, possibly given a lot of money. The buzzing of paparazzi begins in their poor ears. They are feted, lauded, whisked about the world. Us old ones, who have seen it all, are sorry for this neophyte, who has no idea of what is really happening.

He, she, is flattered, pleased.

But ask in a year's time what he or she is thinking—I've heard them: "This is the worst thing that could have happened to me," they say. ▶

On Not Winning the Nobel Prize *(continued)*

Some much-publicized new writers haven't written again, or haven't written what they wanted to, meant to.

And we, the old ones, want to whisper into those innocent ears: "Have you still got your space? Your soul, your own and necessary place where your own voices may speak to you, you alone, where you may dream. Oh, hold onto it, don't let it go."

My mind is full of splendid memories of Africa which I can revive and look at whenever I want. How about those sunsets, gold and purple and orange, spreading across the sky at evening. How about butterflies and moths and bees on the aromatic bushes of the Kalahari? Or, sitting on the pale grassy banks of the Zambesi, the water dark and glossy, with all the birds of Africa darting about. Yes, elephants, giraffes, lions and the rest, there were plenty of those, but how about the sky at night, still unpolluted, black and wonderful, full of restless stars.

There are other memories too. A young African man, eighteen perhaps, in tears, standing in what he hopes will be his "library." A visiting American seeing that his library had no books, had sent a crate of them. The young man had taken each one out, reverently, and wrapped them in plastic. "But," we say, "these books were sent to be read, surely?" "No," he replies, "they will get dirty, and where will I get any more?"

This young man wants us to send him books from England to use as teaching guides.

"I only did four years in senior school," he says, "but they never taught me to teach."

I have seen a teacher in a school where there were no textbooks, not even a chalk for the blackboard. He taught his class of six- to eighteen-year-olds by moving stones in the dust, chanting "Two times two is . . ." and so on. I have seen a girl, perhaps not more than twenty, also lacking textbooks, exercise books, biros, seen her teach the ABCs by scratching the letters in the dirt with a stick, while the sun beat down and the dust swirled.

We are witnessing here that great hunger for education in Africa, anywhere in the Third World, or whatever we call parts of the world where parents long to get an education for their children which will take them out of poverty.

I would like you to imagine yourselves somewhere in southern

Africa, standing in an Indian store, in a poor area, in a time of bad drought. There is a line of people, mostly women, with every kind of container for water. This store gets a bowser of precious water every afternoon from the town, and here the people wait.

The Indian is standing with the heels of his hands pressed down on the counter, and he is watching a black woman, who is bending over a wadge of paper that looks as if it has been torn from a book. She is reading *Anna Karenin*.

She is reading slowly, mouthing the words. It looks a difficult book. This is a young woman with two little children clutching at her legs. She is pregnant. The Indian is distressed, because the young woman's headscarf, which should be white, is yellow with dust. Dust lies between her breasts and on her arms. This man is distressed because of the lines of people, all thirsty. He doesn't have enough water for them. He is angry because he knows there are people dying out there, beyond the dust clouds. His older brother had been here holding the fort, but he had said he needed a break, had gone into town, really rather ill, because of the drought.

This man is curious. He says to the young woman, "What are you reading?"

"It is about Russia," says the girl.

"Do you know where Russia is?" He hardly knows himself.

The young woman looks straight at him, full of dignity, though her eyes are red from dust. "I was best in the class. My teacher said I was best."

The young woman resumes her reading. She wants to get to the end of the paragraph.

The Indian looks at the two little children and reaches for some Fanta, but the mother says, "Fanta makes them thirstier."

The Indian knows he shouldn't do this, but he reaches down to a great plastic container beside him, behind the counter, and pours out two mugs of water, which he hands to the children. He watches while the girl looks at her children drinking, her mouth moving. He gives her a mug of water. It hurts him to see her drinking it, so painfully thirsty is she.

Now she hands him her own plastic water container, which he fills. The young woman and the children watch him closely so that he doesn't spill any. ▶

On Not Winning the Nobel Prize *(continued)*

She is bending again over the book. She reads slowly. The paragraph fascinates her and she reads it again.

Varenka, with her white kerchief over her black hair, surrounded by the children and gaily and good-humouredly busy with them, and at the same visibly excited at the possibility of an offer of marriage from a man she cared for, looked very attractive. Koznyshev walked by her side and kept casting admiring glances at her. Looking at her, he recalled all the delightful things he had heard from her lips, all the good he knew about her, and became more and more conscious that the feeling he had for her was something rare, something he had felt but once before, long, long ago, in his early youth. The joy of being near her increased step by step, and at last reached such a point that, as he put a huge birch mushroom with a slender stalk and up-curling top into her basket, he looked into her eyes and, noting the flush of glad and frightened agitation that suffused her face, he was confused himself, and in silence gave her a smile that said too much.

This lump of print is lying on the counter, together with some old copies of magazines, some pages of newspapers with pictures of girls in bikinis.

It is time for the woman to leave the haven of the Indian store and set off back along the four miles to her village. Outside, the lines of waiting women clamor and complain. But still the Indian lingers. He knows what it will cost this girl—going back home, with the two clinging children. He would give her the piece of prose that so fascinates her, but he cannot really believe this splinter of a girl with her great belly can really understand it.

Why is perhaps a third of *Anna Karenin* here on this counter in a remote Indian store? It is like this.

A certain high official, from the United Nations as it happens, bought a copy of this novel in a bookshop before he set out on his journey to cross several oceans and seas. On the plane, settled in his business class seat, he tore the book into three parts. He looked around his fellow passengers as he did this, knowing he would see looks of shock, curiosity, but some of amusement. When he was settled, his seat belt tight, he said aloud to whomever could hear, "I always do this when I've a long trip. You don't want to have to hold up some heavy great book." The novel was a paperback, but, true, it is a long book. This man is well used to people listening when he spoke. "I always do this, traveling," he confided. "Traveling at all these days, is hard enough." And as soon as people were settling down, he opened his part of *Anna Karenin*, and read. When people looked his way, curiously or not, he confided in them. "No, it really is the only way to travel." He knew the novel, liked it, and this original mode of reading did add spice to what was after all a well-known book.

When he reached the end of a section of the book, he called the air hostess, and sent the chapters back to his secretary, traveling in the cheaper seats. This caused much interest, condemnation, certainly curiosity, every time a section of the great Russian novel arrived, mutilated but readable, in the back part of the plane. Altogether, this clever way of reading Anna *Karenin* makes an impression, and probably no one there would forget it.

Meanwhile, in the Indian store, the young woman is holding on to the counter, her little children clinging to her skirts. She wears jeans, since she is a modern woman, but over them she has put on the heavy woolen skirt, part of the traditional dress of her people: her children can easily cling onto its thick folds.

She sends a thankful look to the Indian, whom she knew liked her and was sorry for her, and she steps out into the blowing clouds.

The children are past crying, and their throats are full of dust.

This was hard, oh yes, it was hard, this stepping, one foot after another, through the dust that lay in soft deceiving mounds under her feet. Hard, but she was used to hardship, was she not? Her mind was on the story she had been reading. She was thinking, She is just like me, in her white headscarf, and she is looking after children too. I could be her, that Russian girl. And the man there, he loves her and will ask her to marry him. She had not finished more than that one paragraph. Yes, she thinks, a man will come for me and take me away from all this, take me and the children, yes, he will love me and look after me.

She steps on. The can of water is heavy on her shoulders. On ▶

On Not Winning the Nobel Prize *(continued)*

she goes. The children can hear the water slopping about. Halfway she stops, sets down the can.

Her children are whimpering and touching it. She thinks that she cannot open it, because dust would blow in. There is no way she can open the can until she gets home.

"Wait," she tells her children, "wait."

She has to pull herself together and go on.

She thinks, My teacher said there is a library, bigger than the supermarket, a big building and it is full of books. The young woman is smiling as she moves on, the dust blowing in her face. I am clever, she thinks. Teacher said I am clever. The cleverest in the school—she said I was. My children will be clever, like me. I will take them to the library, the place full of books, and they will go to school, and they will be teachers—my teacher told me I could be a teacher. My children will live far from here, earning money. They will live near the big library and enjoy a good life.

You may ask how that piece of the Russian novel ever ended up on that counter in the Indian store?

It would make a pretty story. Perhaps someone will tell it.

On goes that poor girl, held upright by thoughts of the water she will give her children once home, and drink a little of herself. On she goes, through the dreaded dusts of an African drought.

We are a jaded lot, we in our threatened world. We are good for irony and even cynicism. Some words and ideas we hardly use, so worn out have they become. But we may want to restore some words that have lost their potency.

We have a treasure-house of literature, going back to the Egyptians, the Greeks, the Romans. It is all there, this wealth of literature, to be discovered again and again by whoever is lucky enough to come upon it. A treasure. Suppose it did not exist. How impoverished, how empty we would be.

We own a legacy of languages, poems, histories, and it is not one that will ever be exhausted. It is there, always.

We have a bequest of stories, tales from the old storytellers, some of whose names we know but some not. The storytellers go back and back, to a clearing in the forest where a great fire burns, and the old shamans dance and sing, for our heritage of stories began in fire, magic, the spirit world. And that is where it is held today.

Ask any modern storyteller and they will say there is always a moment when they are touched with fire, with what we like to call inspiration, and this goes back and back to the beginning of our race, to the great winds that shaped us and our world.

The storyteller is deep inside every one of us. The story-maker is always with us. Let us suppose our world is ravaged by war, by the horrors that we all of us easily imagine. Let us suppose floods wash through our cities, the seas rise. But the storyteller will be there, for it is our imaginations which shape us, keep us, create us—for good and for ill. It is our stories that will recreate us, when we are torn, hurt, even destroyed. It is the storyteller, the dream-maker, the myth-maker, that is our phoenix, that represents us at our best, and at our most creative.

That poor girl trudging through the dust, dreaming of an education for her children, do we think that we are better than she is—we, stuffed full of food, our cupboards full of clothes, stifling in our superfluities?

I think it is that girl, and the women who were talking about books and an education when they had not eaten for three days, that may yet define us. ∿

Have You Read?
More by Doris Lessing

THE GOLDEN NOTEBOOK

Widely considered one of the most
influential novels of the twentieth century,
The Golden Notebook tells the story of
Anna Wulf, a writer who records the
threads of her life in four separate
notebooks. As she attempts to integrate
those fragmented chronicles into one
golden notebook, Anna gives voice to the
challenges of identity-building in a chaotic
world. Known for its literary innovation,
The Golden Notebook brilliantly captures
the anxieties and possibilities of an era
with a vitality that continues to leave its
mark on each new generation of readers.

ESSENTIAL DORIS LESSING CD: EXCERPTS FROM *THE GOLDEN NOTEBOOK* READ BY THE AUTHOR

ALFRED & EMILY

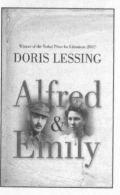

In this extraordinary book, Lessing offers a
moving meditation on parents and
children, war and memory, as she explores
the lives of her parents, two individuals
irrevocably damaged by the Great War. In
the fictional first half of *Alfred & Emily*,
Lessing imagines the happier lives her
parents might have led had there been no
war. This is followed by a piercing
examination of their relationship as it
actually was in the shadow of the war, the
family's move to Africa, and the impact of

their strained union on their daughter, a young woman growing up in a strange land.

TIME BITES: VIEWS AND REVIEWS

In this collection of the very best of Doris Lessing's essays, we are treated to the wisdom and keen insight of a writer who has learned, over the course of a brilliant career spanning more than half a century, to read the world differently. From imagining the secret sex life of Tolstoy to the secrets of Sufism, from reviews of classic books to commentaries on world politics, these essays cover an impressive range of subjects, cultures, periods, and themes, yet they are remarkably consistent in one key regard: Lessing's clear-eyed vision and clearly expressed prose.

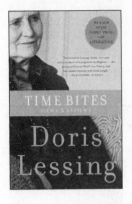

THE CLEFT

In the last years of his life, a contemplative Roman senator embarks on one last epic endeavor: to retell the history of human creation and reveal the little-known story of the Clefts, an ancient community of women living in an Edenic coastal wilderness. The Clefts have neither need nor knowledge of men; childbirth is controlled through the cycles of the moon, and they bear only female children. But with the unheralded birth of a strange new child—a boy—the harmony of their community is suddenly thrown into jeopardy.

In this fascinating and beguiling novel, Lessing confronts the themes that inspired much of her early writing: how men and women manage to live side by side in the world and how the troublesome particulars of gender affect every aspect of our existence.

MARA AND DANN

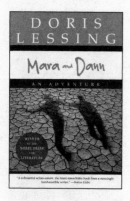

Thousands of years in the future, all the northern hemisphere is buried under the ice and snow of a new Ice Age. At the southern end of a large landmass called Ifrik, two children of the Mahondi people, seven-year-old Mara and her younger brother, Dann, are abducted from their home in the middle of the night. Raised as outsiders in a poor rural village, Mara and Dann learn to survive the hardships and dangers of a life threatened as much by an unforgiving climate and menacing animals as by a hostile community of Rock People. Eventually they join the great human migration North, away from the drought that is turning the southern land to dust and in search of a place with enough water and food to support human life. Traveling across the continent, the siblings enter cities rife with crime, power struggles, and corruption, learning as much about human nature as about how societies function. With a clear-eyed vision of the human condition, *Mara and Dann* is imaginative fiction at its best.

THE STORY OF GENERAL DANN AND MARA'S DAUGHTER, GRIOT AND THE SNOW DOG

Dann is grown up now, hunting for knowledge and despondent over the inadequacies of his civilization. With his trusted companions—Mara's daughter, his hope for the future; the abandoned child-soldier Griot, who discovers the meaning of love and the ability to sing stories; and the snow dog, a faithful friend who brings him back from the depths of despair—Dann embarks on a strange and captivating adventure in a suddenly colder, more watery climate in the north.

THE GRANDMOTHERS: FOUR SHORT NOVELS

In the title novel, two friends fall in love with each other's teenage sons, and these passions last for years, until the women end them, vowing to have a respectable old age. In *Victoria and the Staveneys*, a young woman gives birth to a child of mixed race and struggles with feelings of estrangement as her daughter gets drawn into a world of white privilege. *The Reason for It* traces the birth, faltering, and decline of an ancient culture, with enlightening modern resonances. *A Love Child* features a World War II soldier who believes he has fathered a love child during a fleeting wartime romance and cannot be convinced otherwise.

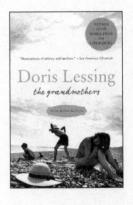

THE SWEETEST DREAM

Frances Lennox ladles out dinner every night to the motley, exuberant, youthful crew assembled around her hospitable table: her two sons and their friends, girlfriends, ex-friends, and fresh-off-the-street friends. It's the early 1960s and certainly "everything is for the best in the best of all possible worlds." Except financial circumstances demand that Frances and her sons live with her proper ex-mother-in-law. And her ex-husband, Comrade Johnny, has just dumped his second wife's problem child at Frances's feet. And the world's political landscape has suddenly become surreal beyond imagination. . . .

Have You Read? *(continued)*

Set against the backdrop of the decade that changed the world forever, *The Sweetest Dream* is a riveting look at a group of people who dared to dream—and faced the inevitable cleanup afterward—from one of the greatest writers of our time.

BEN, IN THE WORLD

At eighteen, Ben is in the world, but not of it. He is too large, too awkward, too inhumanly made. Now estranged from his family, he must find his own path in life. From London and the south of France to Brazil and the mountains of the Andes, Ben is tossed about in a tumultuous search for his people, a reason for his being. How the world receives him, and how he fares in it, will horrify and captivate until the novel's dramatic finale.

LOVE, AGAIN

Love, Again tells the story of a sixty-five-year-old woman who falls in love and struggles to maintain her sanity. Widowed for many years, with grown children, Sarah is a writer who works in the theater in London. During the production of a play, she falls in love with a seductive young actor, the beautiful and androgynous twenty-eight-year-old Bill, and then with the more mature thirty-five-year-old director Henry. Finding herself in a state of longing and desire that she had thought was the province of younger women, Sarah is compelled to explore and examine her own personal history of love, from her earliest childhood desires to her most recent obsessions. The result is a brilliant anatomy of love from a master of human psychology who remains one of the most daring writers of fiction at work today.

UNDER MY SKIN: VOLUME ONE OF MY AUTOBIOGRAPHY, TO 1949

The experiences absorbed through these "skins too few" are evoked in this memoir of Doris Lessing's childhood and youth as the daughter of a British colonial family in Persia and Southern Rhodesia. Honestly and with overwhelming immediacy, Lessing maps the growth of her consciousness, her sexuality, and her politics. *Under My Skin*, winner of the Los Angeles Times Book Prize for Biography, offers a rare opportunity to discover the forces that shaped one of the most distinguished writers of our time.

WALKING IN THE SHADE: VOLUME TWO OF MY AUTOBIOGRAPHY—1949–1962

The second volume of Doris Lessing's extraordinary autobiography covers the years 1949–62, from her arrival in war-weary London with her son, Peter, and the manuscript for her first novel, *The Grass Is Singing*, under her arm, to the publication of her most famous work of fiction, *The Golden Notebook*. She describes how communism dominated the intellectual life of the 1950s and how she, like nearly all communists, became disillusioned with extreme and rhetorical politics and left communism behind. Evoking the bohemian days of a young writer and single mother, Lessing speaks openly about her writing process, her friends

and lovers, her involvement in the theater, and her political activities.

THE REAL THING: STORIES AND SKETCHES

The stories and sketches in this collection penetrate to the heart of human experience with the passion and intelligence readers have come to expect of Doris Lessing. Most of the pieces are set in contemporary London, a city the author loves for its variety, its diversity, its transitoriness, the way it connects the life of animals and birds in the parks to the streets. Lessing's fiction also explores the darker corners of relationships between women and men, as in the rich and emotionally complex title story, in which she uncovers a more parlous reality behind the facade of the most conventional relationship between the sexes.

AFRICAN LAUGHTER

Based on her memories of growing up in Southern Rhodesia and the experiences of four visits to Zimbabwe in the 1980s and 1990s, *African Laughter* is Lessing's poignant study of the homeland from which she was exiled for twenty-five years. With rich detail and intimate understanding, she tackles the role that changing racial and social dynamics, the onslaught of AIDS, political corruption, and ecological factors have played in Zimbabwe's evolution from colonial territory to modern nation.

PRISONS WE CHOOSE TO LIVE INSIDE: ESSAYS

With her signature candor and clarity, Lessing explores new ways to view ourselves and the society we live in, and gives us fresh answers to such enduring questions as how to think for ourselves and how to understand what we know.

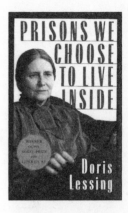

IN PURSUIT OF THE ENGLISH: A DOCUMENTARY

In Pursuit of the English is a novelist's account of a lusty, quarrelsome, unscrupulous, funny, pathetic, full-blooded life in a working-class rooming house. It is a shrewd and unsentimental picture of Londoners you've probably never met or even read about—though they are the real English.

The truth of her perception shines through the pages of a work that is a brilliant piece of cultural interpretation, an intriguing memoir and a thoroughly engaging read.

GOING HOME: A MEMOIR

Going Home is Doris Lessing's account of her first journey back to Africa, the land in which she grew up and in which so much of her emotion and her concern are still invested. Returning to Southern Rhodesia in 1956, she found that her love of Africa had remained as strong as her hatred of the idea of "white supremacy" espoused by its ruling class. *Going Home* evokes brilliantly the experience of the people, black and white, who have shaped and will shape a beloved country.

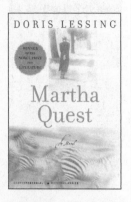

MARTHA QUEST

Intelligent, sensitive, and fiercely passionate, Martha Quest is a young woman living on a farm in Africa, feeling her way through the torments of adolescence and early womanhood. She is a romantic idealistic in revolt against the puritan snobbery of her parents, trying to live to the fullest with every nerve, emotion, and instinct laid bare to experience. For her, this is a time of solitary reading, daydreams, dancing—and the first disturbing encounters with sex. *Martha Quest* is the first novel in Doris Lessing's classic Children of Violence series of novels, each a masterpiece in its own right and, taken together, an incisive and all-encompassing vision of our world in the twentieth century.

A PROPER MARRIAGE

An unconventional woman trapped in a conventional marriage, Martha Quest struggles to maintain her dignity and her sanity through the misunderstandings, frustrations, infidelities, and degrading violence of a failing marriage. Finally, she must make the heartbreaking choice of whether to sacrifice her child as she turns her back on marriage and security.

A Proper Marriage is the second novel in the Children of Violence series.

A RIPPLE FROM THE STORM

Martha Quest, the heroine of the Children of Violence series, has been acclaimed as one of the greatest fictional creations in the English language. In *A Ripple from the Storm*, Doris Lessing charts Martha Quest's personal and political adventures in race-torn British Africa, following Martha through World War II, a grotesque second marriage, and an excursion into Communism. This wise and starling novel perceptively reveals the paradoxes, passions, and ironies rooted in the life of twentieth-century Anglo-Africa.

A Ripple from the Storm is the third novel in the Children of Violence series.

LANDLOCKED

In the aftermath of World War II, Martha Quest finds herself completely disillusioned. She is losing faith in the Communist movement in Africa, and her marriage to one of the movement's leaders is disintegrating. Determined to resist the erosion of her personality, she engages in her first satisfactory love affair and breaks free, if only momentarily, from her suffocating unhappiness.

Landlocked is the fourth novel in the Children of Violence series.

THE FOUR-GATED CITY

Now middle-aged, Martha Quest moves to London, where she lives through many of the great social and political movements of the second half of the twentieth century. In Lessing's chilling rendition, though, that century ends with the nuclear decimation of World War III.

The Four-Gated City is the fifth and final novel in the Children of Violence series.

Don't miss the next book by your favorite author. Sign up now for AuthorTracker by visiting www.AuthorTracker.com.